"I will be right by you. It is daunting to face the unknown, but challenges feel so good when accomplished."

Inspiring words. That didn't quite make Cady want to race forward and dodge under the rotating propeller. But when she placed her hand in his and he clasped her fingers firmly, something inside her sparked. It was as if she'd just touched a smoldering fire and wanted to ease in a little closer to allow it to envelope her. *You can do this.*

"Good, *oui*?" He maintained eye contact with her. Soft brown irises twinkled. Mischievous. And sensual. She felt that gaze in her core and her inner wild child wanted to grab him and kiss him silly.

Seriously?

Yes. But she wasn't that careless. Especially not when on the clock.

Very well. Today she would step far outside her comfort zone. And to do it while holding this man's hand? It could be good.

It *would* be good.

"Let's do this," Cady said with not as much enthusiasm as was required, but with enough to keep from fainting. For now.

Dear Reader,

My story ideas always start with a hero and heroine. Sometimes I know their professions; other times it's more organic and that information fits itself in during the first draft. I am a very visual person, so I like to collect images to inspire my stories. This one was heavily influenced by putting together random photos and writing around what those images had to say. I always write with those images close at hand. Sometimes they just start talking to me, and away we go!

Stories are funny like that. But I always follow wherever they lead. Even if it's a whirlwind trip to Finland and then off to Paris! Along the way I fall in love with the people at the center of it all. I hope you will, too.

Find inspiration boards for all my books @toastfaery on Pinterest.

Michele

Parisian Escape with the Billionaire

Michele Renae

Recycling programs for this product may not exist in your area.

ISBN-13: 978-1-335-59636-9

Parisian Escape with the Billionaire

For questions and comments about the quality of this book, please contact us at CustomerService@Harlequin.com.

Harlequin Enterprises ULC
22 Adelaide St. West, 41st Floor
Toronto, Ontario M5H 4E3, Canada
www.Harlequin.com

Printed in U.S.A.

Michele Renae is the pseudonym for award-winning author Michele Hauf. She has published over ninety novels in historical, paranormal and contemporary romance and fantasy, as well as written action/adventure as Alex Archer. Instead of "writing what she knows," she prefers to write "what she would love to know and do" (and yes, that includes being a jewel thief and/or a brain surgeon).

You can email Michele at toastfaery@gmail.com.
Instagram: @MicheleHauf
Pinterest: @toastfaery

Books by Michele Renae

Harlequin Romance

Cinderella's Second Chance in Paris
The CEO and the Single Dad

Visit the Author Profile page
at Harlequin.com.

For Lois and Mary because you two are always there, through thick and thin. Love you!

Praise for Michele Renae

"Renae's debut Harlequin [Romance] novel is a later-in-life romance that's sure to tug at readers' heartstrings."

—*Library Journal* on *Cinderella's Second Chance in Paris*

CHAPTER ONE

Arcadia Burton flipped on the lights in the front reception area of Victory Marketing. Sun peeking over the horizon glinted copper across the office's steel structural beams. Even with the holiday season seeing the majority of the employees out on vacation, Cady always liked to get a jump on the day and ensure the reception area was organized and ready to go.

Receptionist Extraordinaire was the title she secretly gave herself. She mastered command central, answering phones, scheduling client meetings, researching assignment locations and making all related preparations should travel be required. Organizing was her wheelhouse. She could not function unless she knew others were happy and satisfied. And working for the top marketing agency in Las Vegas—ranked number three overall in the United States—gave her pride.

From her canvas bag stitched with the phrase Coffee Is My Spirit Animal, Cady pulled out items from a grocery stop she'd made on the drive to work. Refill pods for espresso, coffee and hot chocolate were placed in the cupboard in alphabetical order. Flimsy bamboo stir sticks were artfully arranged in a steel container. Leftover napkins from the holiday party featuring Christmas trees were swirled. The donuts she always stocked were placed under glass. Today she'd brought in her favorite flavor, Blue Suede Banana, and entirely expected she might have to take most of it home with her.

Glancing to her computer screen, she verified only one client arrival today. But he wouldn't stop into the office; rather a liaison would meet him at the airport. Actually, he wasn't a client but a freelance hire. The award-winning photographer, Sabre d'Aramitz, had been hired to do a desert shoot for one of Victory's clients. And since the agency had nabbed the world-famous photographer, they had capitalized by adding a second leg to his assignment, a stopover in Finland to capture the aurora borealis for a different client.

Cady had researched the photographer on his social media. As well, she'd packed a travel bag for the client liaison who would accompany him on his shoot. She had learned Monsieur d'Aramitz liked protein bars as a snack, spring water and beef jerky. While his photographs garnered awards and worldwide recognition, the man himself was a bit of a media evader. Shots of him were rare, unless it was of him deplaning or hopping into an off-road vehicle as he ventured off on another adventure. But a few images had captured him unaware. Talk about drop-dead gorgeous! Coal black hair, usually slicked back over his ears, capped his rugged square face, and dark brows drew attention to intense brown eyes. He usually wore a trimmed beard and moustache, and his skin tone was a natural tan. Or maybe it was from his adventuring. Cady couldn't decide. Didn't matter. The man was all kinds of sexy.

Too bad she wouldn't get to meet him. Or maybe, just as well. She had already concocted a lusty fantasy about dashing off into a wild jungle, swept along on Monsieur d'Aramitz's strong arm. Her frequent daydreams were a product of growing up in a household that demanded she care for herself and make her own happiness. Always left alone? Let that imagination soar! Sexy French photographer? If she saw him today, she might swoon.

"Women don't swoon anymore," she muttered, and gave a perfecting straighten to the business cards set on the reception desk.

A low-key day, then. In fact, only one employee may or may not wander in; the rest of about a dozen agents were still on vacation until the second week in January. Cady had only to ensure the photographer was picked up at the airport by the client liaison and that they made it to the helicopter pad. The rest of the day would be spent going through the Christmas cards from hundreds of companies worldwide, replying to them if thanks were necessary for some elaborate corporate gift. Whoever had sent the chocolates from France would definitely receive a grateful note. She had eaten two of the truffles and she was pretty sure each had taken up permanent residence on her not-so-slender hips.

Taking advantage of the peace and calm, she popped an apple cider pod into the brewing machine. Cinnamon and apple suffused the air. She settled onto her chair behind the massive half-circle marble reception desk.

The phone rang. Punching a button to answer the call via the computer she said, "Good morning, this is Victory Marketing. How may I direct your call?"

"Cady, this is Lynn."

Lynn Marshall was one of two client liaisons who alternated shifts. Treating clients as if they were kings or queens was their key focus, but also ensuring Victory Marketing's dollars were being properly utilized. Even though they were basically glorified handlers, it was a dream job that involved lots of travel. The other liaison was on maternity leave after giving birth on Christmas morning to a sweet baby girl.

Something felt off about this call. Or rather, *sounded* off.

"Oh, Lynn, you sound..."

"Like I have the cold of the century and I can't breathe through my nose?"

"That's it."

A moan lumbered across the connection.

"But the shoot with Monsieur d'Aramitz is today," Cady said, perhaps a bit too accusingly. She adjusted her tone to a polite firmness. "He's due to arrive in less than an hour."

"I know," Lynn said. *Know* coming out as *doe.*

Cady frowned, feeling the woman's pain as a twinge in her temple. Things could not go wrong on her watch. How to fix this?

"I need your help, Cady."

"Anything," she responded by rote. Her job was, after all, to make sure everyone was happy.

Helping was her thing. You need a thousand-page report printed and bound within an hour? Just ask Cady. Car ran out of gas on the way to work? Cady will hop in her reliable car and come to the rescue with a full gas can in the trunk. You can't seem to get your party-ravaged bloodshot eyes to look less vampirish with a client meeting in ten minutes? Cady has the eye drops for that.

"You need to pick up the photographer from the airport," Lynn said, "and accompany him on the shoot. Sabre d'Aramitz is a world-class artist. The Wonder Maverick, Cady! I can't believe my body is doing this to me today."

The Wonder Maverick was the label the press had given the man who was known for capturing wonder in the simplest of things. He focused on nature—from macro shots of insects and small animals to long-shot scenery in the most exotic of locations. He had traveled the world and had been awarded countless times. The National Geographic had labeled him one of the top ten photographers of the century.

"But, Lynn, I've never—" Cady bit her lower lip.

An opportunity to get out of the office and spend the day with a sexy photographer? Rev up those fantasies! But no. Certainly, any interaction with the man must be for business. No swooning allowed. Besides, she'd get to step into Lynn's shoes, learn her part of the job. Adding skills to her résumé was never a bad thing. Maybe she could work her way toward a promotion should the other liaison decide to stay home permanently? She did have a mortgage, and bills were always a challenge to cover each month. Was it her fault retail therapy was her one means to lifting her spirits?

"You have to do this, Cady. Everyone else is out, and Lisa is nursing a newborn."

Yes, and Cady had picked up on Lisa's body language the past few months. That woman was a nurturing mother. She suspected she may not return after maternity leave. Which meant her liaison position would be open.

"And I trust you," Lynn continued. "You're kind and smart, and you have a manner about you. You are present but you never get in anyone's way. That's what is needed for this job. You have to accompany Monsieur d'Aramitz, be by his side, make sure he has everything he needs. But don't get in his hair. Can you do that?"

It sounded simple enough. She had nothing of import to do in the office today. *Not* get in his hair? But it was so dark and looked absolutely caressable.

"Cady?" Lynn's voice croaked. "Tell me you can be at the airport in forty-five minutes."

It was a fifteen-minute drive from the office. "I can be there. But, Lynn—"

"No buts, Cady. D'Aramitz is taking photos for one of our biggest clients today."

"Exactly. What if I screw it up?"

"You won't. Besides, you already know half the job. You're the one who packs my duffel when I go on client excursions."

She'd packed for Lynn yesterday afternoon, ensuring she had the essentials like snacks, water, cash, a notebook and a warm jacket for the desert. She'd even tossed in a collapsible hiking pole and some gloves to protect against cacti and sharp rocks. The region they were to shoot in would be cool this January morning, but would warm to sweater weather as the day went on.

"It's basically making the man happy. And that's what you do, right? Cady," Lynn whispered, "I'm dying here. Say something."

Cady smoothed a palm over the sweater she wore. She was prepared. If a bit, gaudily. But she had a coat and kept a pair of walking shocs in her car.

"Of course, you can depend on me, Lynn. I'll meet Monsieur d'Aramitz at the airport."

"Thank goodness. I promise I'll be better by tomorrow so I can accompany him to Finland. I wouldn't miss that trip for the world." She coughed and moaned. "Oh, misery. The helicopter will be waiting for both of you."

Helicopter? Cady's heart landed in her gut with a splash.

Right. A helicopter would drop them off in the middle of the desert, as requested by the photographer. Sounded adventurous and exciting and... Cady had never flown before. Not even on an airplane. She didn't like being out of control. Of knowing she couldn't stop the vehicle and get out anytime she wished. And the idea of getting inside a flying bubble with a swiveling blade on top of it...

"I'll take your silence as a good sign," Lynn

rasped. "I'm going to drown myself in cough syrup now. Pray for me, Cady." The connection clicked off.

"Pray for you?" Cady mumbled. "What about me? I have to board a helicopter in an hour and do it without losing my cookies all over an important client."

Closing her eyes tightly, Cady mined the fortitude that had always nudged her forward in any situation that felt hopeless. So many opportunities to learn survival growing up with her mother and her endless stream of boyfriends, lovers and husbands. Cady had learned it was always better to make sure others were happy and satisfied than to suffer the brunt of their anger or unhappiness. When times got tough, Cady rose to the challenge. Taking care of her own meals when she was five? She'd managed. Getting herself to school events across town when she was ten? Learning how to take the city bus had been mastered.

Climbing inside a helicopter for an important client?

"You can do this."

Time to snatch this opportunity and show them Cady Burton was worthy of a promotion.

The flight from New York had landed twenty minutes ago and now Sabre collected his baggage. According to the schedule the liaison had texted him last night a car would be waiting curbside. Standard.

He flung a black duffel over a shoulder and picked up the canvas bag that contained his camera and gear. Then he set it down and blew out a breath. A deep inhale, and then another heavy exhale. The flight across the ocean from Paris and then direct from New York to Las Vegas had been long, but over years of traveling he'd trained himself to take advantage of the downtime and sleep. And when not sleeping, he used his time to proof his work on the laptop. He rarely experienced jet lag, no matter which direction across the globe he traveled.

But he was feeling *something* right now. Not exhaustion. Some stretches and fascia massage had restored any lethargy he'd felt upon deplaning. The sensation of…being out of place, airy and not moored skittered through his veins and made him antsy. Nerves?

Honestly? Yes. It had been six months since he, a certified nomad, had booked a job. Six months since he'd set foot on the scene, whether it be media, social, entertainment or yachting with his family.

Six months since his *grand-père*, Gaston d'Aramitz, had passed away.

It felt as if he had just lost him yesterday. And yet it also felt as if a thousand years had passed since Sabre had carried the coffin, along with his two brothers, to the family mausoleum in Père Lachaise. The old man was gone. The most important person in Sabre's life.

And now Sabre was alone.

He was a nomad. Alone was his natural mode. But this was a different sort of alone. It was as if he'd been abandoned by something so personal.

Sabre had family. His father was currently in Marseilles doing—well, Sabre didn't know and didn't particularly care. Pierre d'Aramitz rarely communicated with Sabre beyond to update him on his travels. And his two brothers were both in Paris at the moment. Jacques, the oldest, was generally too busy to remember he had two younger brothers who might like to share a beer once in a while. And Blaise, the youngest, had just broken up with an actress, or so Sabre had learned from the airline's news stream when he'd first boarded at Charles de Gaulle. They were not a close family. Which lent itself to the shape of his lifestyle. He'd always been good with being on his own, standing on the periphery, looking in.

Gaston d'Aramitz had been Sabre's only real connection to love and knowing what acceptance and pride felt like. Grand-père had been the one to place a camera in Sabre's hands when he was young and teach him how to see the world through the lens.

Gaston d'Aramitz had been an award-winning

nature photographer. He had walked the soil in nearly all countries, eaten the food, shared his knowledge and in turn had taken in new knowledge. When not traveling, he had given Sabre his time and attention. The world would never be the same without him in it.

But what the hell? With an abrupt lift of his chin, Sabre caught himself from going full-on maudlin. He would not break down in an airport. Been there, done that. Privately, at his Paris penthouse. This was the life he had made for himself. A life of adventure, travel, wonder and respect for all natural things. A life…that would forever see him alone and venturing. Would he ever find a companion to walk alongside him? Sabre doubted such a dream would come to fruition. He'd yet to have a long-term romance that didn't end in the woman fleeing his vagabond lifestyle.

So he accepted, for the most part, his aloneness. And now he'd have to incorporate this new alone into his shape of the world. Time to move forward by honoring the gift he'd been given by his *grand-père.*

And so, Las Vegas it was. Victory Marketing had hired him to capture some desert shots for an environmental client. Then the second leg of his assignment would fly him to Oulu, Finland,

and on to Kemi to capture the aurora borealis for a feature in a science magazine.

Nothing overly challenging. No death-defying excursions required. He could do this. This was his wheelhouse.

"This one's for you, Grand-père. Watch over me. I love you."

Sabre picked up his bags and wandered out to the sidewalk.

It didn't take long to spot the sign with his name on it. Because it was held by a woman with stunning red hair. Bouncy and lush, it looked like carnelian glinting in the pale morning light. Sabre had never seen such gorgeous hair. The image of him nuzzling his face against her hair, losing himself in it all, flashed not so briefly across his thoughts. Dating had also gone by the wayside these past six months. So to feel something like a normal sexual stirring just by glancing at a beautiful woman gave him some hope that he might actually surface from his grief.

He was brought back to the moment when she dipped her head shyly and approached him. "Monsieur d'Aramitz?"

Was she the handler who was supposed to accompany him on the shoot? A woman who embodied lush goddess curves. What a bombshell. Life had just looked up.

"*Oui.*" He stepped in to buss her on both cheeks

and in the process inhaled a soft scent reminiscent of fresh-cut apples. "Delicious."

"What was that?"

Don't let a pretty head of hair distract you.

"Uh? Oh." He stepped back and winced. *What the hell, d'Aramitz? Get your head in the game.* This job was important. He couldn't allow the world to think he'd lost his touch. That losing his *grand-père* had thoroughly devastated him.

"I am Sabre d'Aramitz," he said. "And you are?"

"Arcadia Burton." She offered her hand and he shook it. When in America… "You can call me Cady. Lynn Marshall was supposed to accompany you today but she's not feeling well so I'll be taking her place. The car is right here. The helicopter—" she swallowed noticeably. A bit of nerves? "—is waiting for us."

"Then lead on." Sabre tossed his bags in the open trunk and opened the back car door for her. Now he noticed she wore dark pants and a curious sweater with white snowflakes against a blue background. He slid in after her and the car rolled away from the curb. "Snowflakes in Las Vegas?"

"Huh? Oh. I'm so sorry, I didn't dress for such a job today. I thought I'd be alone in the office, so the intention was to get all the use out of this party sweater I could."

"It is festive."

"You haven't seen anything yet." She tugged

at the hem of her sweater and suddenly it lit up, the snowflakes twinkling. She gave another tug. "Sorry. I promise I'm not weird."

Sabre laughed. "Well, it is Las Vegas, *oui*? If you can't work the flashing lights, then you do not belong."

"Exactly!" Her cheeks brightened to a rosy blush.

Not stuffy and even a little quirky? He had hit the jackpot. And in Vegas, of all places! "You'll have to allow me to photograph you in all your twinkling glory, later. It is quite a marvel."

"I'm not sure if you're teasing me or being serious."

Teasing or *flirting*, he silently corrected. Maybe a little of both? He wasn't a man to check his words or put up his guard. He acted, he reacted, he lived whatever life tossed at him. And if he had to spend the day with this beautiful woman, alone in the desert? It would be more pleasant than he had expected it to be.

"Here's to a belated Christmas present," he said as he watched the passing casinos on the Las Vegas strip.

And he wasn't referring to that hideous sweater as a present. No, he'd been gifted the company of an utterly gorgeous woman whose only job was to make sure his every need was met.

CHAPTER TWO

THE BARITONE *WHUMP* of the helicopter propeller beating the air felt as if it were punching Cady's chest. She stood just inside the hangar while Monsieur d'Aramitz and the pilot loaded the bags and gear. For a moment, she allowed in a distraction from the death-defying excursion she was about to attempt by observing the tall photographer. He wore a dark brown canvas jacket and khaki pants, along with black leather gloves, and moved with the grace of a panther. Ready for adventure.

Gripping her fingers tightly in fists, Cady closed her eyes. The thud of her heartbeats overwhelmed the noise from the helicopter. She. Could. Not. Do. This.

Never had she flown. It wasn't so much a fear as a rational will to keep her feet on the ground and stay alive. Accidents happened all the time. Whole flights went down over massive oceans. People got lost on desert islands and were forced to live on coconuts. What was wrong with safety first?

Her mother would always chuckle when Cady swore she'd never fly.

"Then you'll never have an interesting life," Maria Burton would taunt. "You have to leave Las Vegas sooner or later, Arcadia. Toss a little careless into your careful ways. There's more to life than making coffee for the office nerds and booking rooms for visiting clients."

"Yes, but at least the life I live is grounded and not based on the validation of rich men," Cady muttered now, thinking about how her mother sought love only in the eyes of a man with a fat wallet. And if he'd hit it big at the poker table? Now that was Maria Burton's kind of man.

Cady was careful. For good reason. Careless had gotten her mother in too deep far too many times.

But enough excuses. Her mother's taste in men had nothing to do with this moment. She stood on the precipice of adventure. Something she'd often dreamed about. And now was her chance to show she had what it took to do the job. No time to wimp out.

A gorgeous man, *seriously* gorgeous, who spoke with a French accent that could melt her at the knees and reduce her to a puddle, stalked toward her, a grin on his face. He looked like a kid excited for a playground ride. A dangerous one made of metal, seared by the hot sun, and set to circle endlessly at ridiculous speeds.

His enthusiasm bounced him up to her. "Ready?" Sabre asked. "I've not flown in this type of helicopter before. It's smaller, but quieter, and with the surround glass the view will be spectacular."

Cady swallowed. Her knees melted. And not because of all the enthusiastic sexiness standing before her. Surround glass and a spectacular view from thousands of feet in the air did not sound like a party she wanted to attend.

"I'm not sure..." she started.

Stop right there, Fraidy Cady.

What was she doing? Precipice, remember? If she could manage this small adventure, then it could only lead to bigger and better. Certainly, she couldn't send the photographer off on his own simply because she was too chicken to fly a few dozen miles out into the desert encased within a bulb of glass. Lynn would be angry. The company's reputation would take a hit. She'd probably get fired. At the very least, any chance at a promotion would be quashed.

And really? Was she just going to allow her mother to be right all the time? Adventure shouldn't have to knock politely; it grabbed a person and whisked them away.

It would be a quick trip, she reasoned. People flew in helicopters all the time. When was the last time she'd heard about an accident, anyway?

Well. There had been that one on the news—stop!

"You have not flown in a helicopter before?" Sabre asked, suddenly serious. His windswept hair tufted at the top of his head, and his collar had blown up against his neck. His beard looked so soft, so touchable. "An airplane?"

Cady shook her head.

"Ah." With a shrug, he offered, "I can go on by myself. It really is not necessary I have a babysitter to do the photography work required. You can wait here until I return, *oui*?"

In her dreams. She needed to keep her job. Having a job paid the bills and the mortgage on her little one-bedroom house too far away from the strip and Victory Marketing. As well, the bags Sabre had already placed on the helicopter included her phone. And...she didn't want to disappoint a client. That was not Cady Burton's style. Foremost, she must keep him happy.

Cady exhaled heavily. Then she wiggled her shoulders and shook out her fingers, forcing her muscles to unclench. "I can do this."

"Of course, you can. It is, how do you say it? Like riding a *velo*?"

"A what?"

"Er, a bicycle. But here." He held out a gloved hand. A wide strong hand with long fingers that she felt sure could hold a woman in all the right ways.

And never let me go.

"I will be right by you. It is daunting to face the unknown, but challenges feel so good when accomplished."

Inspiring words. That didn't quite make Cady want to race forward and dodge under the rotating propeller. But when she placed her hand in his, and he clasped her fingers firmly, something inside her sparked. It was as if she'd just touched a smoldering fire and wanted to ease in a little closer to allow it to envelope her.

You can do this.

"Good, *oui*?" He maintained eye contact with her. Soft brown irises twinkled. Mischievous. And sensual. She felt that gaze in her core and her inner wild child wanted to grab him and kiss him silly.

Seriously?

Yes. But she wasn't that careless. Especially not when on the clock.

Very well. Today, she would step far outside her comfort zone. And to do it while holding this man's hand? It could be good.

It would be good.

"Let's do this," Cady said with not as much enthusiasm as was required, but with enough to keep from fainting. For now.

Sabre set his gear bag on a bench beside a small stone-faced desert way station that had been closed, according to the sign on the window, five years earlier. Bright red paint had faded to pink and was scuffed on one side of the building from blowing sand. The pilot had given him a security code to unlock the door, if need be. Inside were basic provisions and a sat phone to call for help should an emergency arise. But the pilot mentioned he'd been dropping tourists, media and photographers here for years and there hadn't been an incident yet.

Sabre did not expect any such emergency. He was here to photograph colorful sandstone formations in a state park that covered more than forty-thousand acres. The area was swirled, carved and tumescent with red sandstone that varied in tones from bloodred to fire-orange, yellow, ochre and everything in between. Petrified trees pocked the landscape here and there, skeletal remains of long-lost life. And before landing, the pilot had pointed out a petroglyph etched into the side of a sandstone rise that dated back over ten-thousand years.

Within the park, there were marked trails for tourists and hikers, but Sabre had asked to be let off beyond those popular spaces. He'd spend the afternoon snapping shots. The pilot would return just after sunset to pick them up.

Such assignments were his very breath. Though Sabre suspected he wouldn't have to dodge any wild animals or mud bogs this time around. He'd been warned about the big horn sheep, which wandered everywhere. As well, he never went anywhere without a first-aid kit tucked in his pack.

It was the woman he was worried about. She'd been pale as the moon waiting to board the helicopter. And once in the air, she had gripped his hand as if in a vice. He hadn't minded. She had soft hands. Luminous skin. And smelled like apples. Spending the afternoon with her trailing behind him? Not a bad gig.

Grand-père had taught him how to see nature, but the old man had also insisted a man should never resist the opportunity to converse with a woman. Any woman, be she young, old, pretty or plain. The opposite sex was so much stronger and smarter than any man, Gaston would say with reverence. An ode to his beloved wife of fifty years.

Upon exiting their ride, Sabre had given Cady some space. She'd walked around behind the way station and hadn't yet returned. He recalled his first flight when he was five or six. He'd tossed his cookies once they'd reached altitude. He was no man to judge anyone's reaction to such a new experience.

Digging his camera out of the bag, he adjusted the shoulder strap. While he could easily work on his own, he did appreciate a helping hand. He'd give Mademoiselle Burton a task. It would help her feel useful. She didn't seem the precious sort who would grumble about her shoes being uncomfortable or the dusty, dry air or insects. But he wouldn't know what she would be like until they got into it.

When the woman wandered around the side of the building, he smiled at her and winked. The color had returned to her face. The bottle of water she held was half-empty.

"Good?" he asked.

She nodded and tugged the bottom of her sweater, which set the lights to a twinkle. "I'm good."

Sabre laughed. "So it seems."

She tugged the sweater and the lights went out as she joined him. "I survived a helicopter ride," she announced with fanfare. "The rest of the day should be easygoing."

"Depends on whether or not you like hiking."

She shrugged. "Honestly, I had expected to be sitting behind a reception desk today, but now that I've mastered the challenge of flying, I'm so ready for the next adventure. I like hiking. I've got comfy shoes that have seen all-day shopping sprees. And there's a jacket in my duffel, which I'm putting on right now. An afternoon in the desert shouldn't be a problem. I promise I won't get in your way. I'll just stay close and if you need anything, give a holler. I've brought snacks and water. I am here to ensure you are happy."

"I like a woman who plans ahead. And I do

have a task for you." He handed her his pocket notebook, encased in thin aluminum. "I record the latitude and longitude of my shots and any details of note. I used to do it on my phone but I find handwritten is much better, and it's much easier to write than to punch those tiny letters on a screen. Would you mind recording what I tell you to write down?"

"Be happy to. Let's get to work!"

Sabre nodded with satisfaction. Very agreeable woman. Despite the curious sweater, she was appealing. And curvaceous. Cady Burton looked like a real woman, and her sweet smile made him forget that he had been doubtful about taking this assignment. Grand-père would nudge him, and say, "Talk to her, *mon petit-fils*, get to know her."

"There's an interesting outcrop just over there." She pointed. "I think they call it a beehive. Those hive-like structures are all over this park. I love the sandwiched colors in the rise of the rocks. What do you think?"

She did have an artistic eye. The large hive-shaped outcrop also featured a spindly skeleton of a former tree. Perfect.

He started walking and checked the compass on his watch. As he passed Cady, he called out their latitude and longitude. "Got it?"

"Of course!"

Sabre smiled to himself. He'd been dreading

this first venture out on the job after being away from it for six months. He'd suspected thoughts of his *grand-père* would overwhelm him, and that focus would be difficult to maintain. But the astute redhead who trailed behind him distracted his focus just enough.

And *just enough* may be more than enough to get him through this job.

Hours later, Sabre felt he'd gotten the necessary shots. They'd probably hiked three or four miles in a circular manner. Every time they noticed a hiker, he veered in the other direction. They'd landed back at the way station and Cady, who seemed not at all bothered by the walking and his calling out notations, now handed him a bottle of water and a protein bar. His favorite brand, from a sustainable company he had financed. Had someone done some research on him?

"I love the peanut butter ones," she said, taking a bite of her own bar. "Oh, look!" She wandered off, munching and simultaneously pointing at the sky. "I love how the sunset is streaked with pink and gold. It's like jewelry, don't you think?" She glanced at him, a hand to her neck as if to embrace the imagined jewels. "Like I could wrap the sky around me."

After an afternoon of astute notations and frequent comments that she was *here to make you happy, Monsieur d'Aramitz*, his fearful assistant had really loosened up. She had forgotten her rigid need to act as a handler, allowing some of her inner wonder to slip out. Sabre picked up his camera and flicked off a series of shots of the bejeweled sunset. But…why not? He framed Cady into the images as well. Her hair absolutely glowed against the twenty-four-carat sky. And her face beamed. A desert goddess gilding the air with her presence.

"I've never hiked in the desert before. I love this!" With a satisfied sigh, she wandered back to the bench and picked up a water bottle. "Please tell me I didn't get in those shots."

"You made it into all of them."

Her jaw dropped open.

"You mustn't mind. The sunset was singing behind you. And you were the conductor. The two of you made a perfect pair."

With a chuckle, she said, "That kind of talk will get you far, mister."

Far, as in…? Was she flirting with him? He wouldn't have minded that at all. But he had no intention of carrying this further than flirtation. The complications of sex always tugged him in an emotional rope pull. And he was emotionally tapped after the last half a year. Besides, of all the potential romantic involvements, long distance simply did not work for his lifestyle.

"See for yourself." Sabre turned the camera to show her the screen and she bent to take a peek at his work. She smelled even better after hours of walking. It was as if her perfume exuded from within her, sweetening the air.

"Oh." She winced and touched her hair cautiously. Back to the apprehensive traveler, then?

"You don't like the photos?"

"I..." she tugged in the corner of her lower lip with a tooth "...think they're good, actually. I hate having my picture taken. But those..."

Yes, these images enhanced her natural glow. Did she not know she was beautiful? How could she not? Surely, the woman had many suitors or lovers. She was not the sort most men could walk by without looking at twice.

"I will forward them to you," he said. "I promise I won't publish them. Not without a signed waiver. But this job was specific about having no people in the images."

"Right, they're for a sustainability campaign. And I can't remember when I last recycled. Oh, but your work is truly stunning. Our client will be very happy with these images."

"*Merci*."

She had a way of making him feel good, accepted, even. It was disconcerting only because it had been a while since Sabre had been out with others, socialized in any way.

"It's been months since I've been on the job. I have to admit..." He leaned back and opened the protein bar.

"Admit what?" She sat next to him. A careful fold of the empty wrapper and then she tucked it in a pocket of her backpack.

"I was unsure about this shoot today," he admitted. "I haven't worked since my *grand-père*'s death."

"Oh. I'm so sorry. *Grand-père* means grandfather?"

He nodded.

"He must have been special to you?"

"Very." Sabre bit into the protein bar. Never easy to speak out loud his memories of the old man. And yet, right now, he did not feel as if the world were watching The Wonder Maverick, expecting so much from him. Wondering if he would fall in the shadow of his loss or perhaps even lose his touch. "My *grand-père* was everything to me. When he died, he left me his home in the Eighth Arrondissement. Uh...that's in Paris. I haven't been able to visit it, though. Not sure what memories my footsteps will stir up in the dust." He took a few more bites, then his tone brightened, "He gave me my first camera when I was ten and showed me how to find the wonder in the simplest of things."

"Your work shows that wonder. I loved the

rainforest butterfly series you did for National Geographic last year."

Sabre turned toward her. "You know my work?"

"I did some research on you before prepping for today's outing. I always familiarize myself with clients and our freelance hires. You've shot some iconic images. They are truly wondrous."

"That label the press gives me is silly."

"The Wonder Maverick? I kind of like it. It's a little Harry Potter-ish, a bit dark and mysterious but in a fantastical way."

"I like dark and mysterious." He waggled his hands before him as if he were a magician commanding some magic. "Though I've never claimed much mystery. I am an open book who scatters his pages across the globe."

"I think the mystery is in your photos. There's always something that draws the viewer deeper. Back for a second perusal. It's a feeling. An emotion."

He did try to convey emotion in his work, because that was easier than actually doing so with a face-to-face conversation.

Cady laughed and then caught herself with a touch of her fingers to her soft pink lips. "Sorry, that might have been too personal. I enjoyed tagging along with you today. I've always been more of a mental adventurer. This afternoon has been a kick-start to some of my daydreams. Who knows?

I might even look into booking a vacation this spring. But I hope I didn't get in your way."

"Not at all. I've never had such a beautiful assistant."

"Beautiful?"

Her mumbled chuckle made Sabre frown. "You do not believe you are beautiful?"

"Um, maybe…not terrible to look at."

"Wow. You really can't see yourself, can you, Cady?"

She studied him for a moment, her fingers working nervously with the crinkly paper wrapping the plastic water bottle.

"What are you thinking about?" he asked. Because surely, she had gone beyond a protest and was deciding if his words about her beauty could possibly be true.

"Honestly? I was thinking about my mother."

"Ah?" That was not what he'd expected. Especially when he was feeling as though the work portion of the day had come to a close and they were relaxing, getting to know one another. Time to *talk to the woman*, as Grand-père would have coached him.

And yet, she was thinking about her mother?

"Sorry," she said. The way she often brushed her hair over an ear captivated him. "My mother has…a manner about her. With men. Rich men. I know you're quite wealthy. I shouldn't have said anything. I was just feeling like, between us..."

"That we were connecting on a level beyond work?" he suggested.

She nodded. "I shouldn't have brought it up. Please don't tell my boss. This is strictly business. It wouldn't be professional to—well." She shoved the notebook toward him. "Here."

Sabre set it on his lap and then bent to catch her gaze. "You can drop the professional facade. I like talking to you."

"You...you do?"

"*Oui*, but I do feel a bit out of practice with the socializing. I've been a sort of hermit these months since my *grand-père* passed."

"Completely understandable. I would enjoy chatting and getting to know you better. But the sun just flickered out on the horizon. I'm pretty sure the helicopter is on its way to pick us up."

"Of course." It was still twilight and the sky glowed, brightening what might have been a darker evening. Sabre didn't want the day to end just yet. There must be a way he could win a few more hours with her. Just to chat. And take in her beauty. "Are you hungry, Cady?"

"Uh..." She shrugged. "Maybe?"

"I have wondered about those buffets the Americans seem to flock to. So many foods arrayed in a long line under plastic canopies and lit like precious gifts."

Laughter giddied up from her belly. "Are you serious? Those buffets are feeding troughs. Stack your plate high. Eat. Repeat."

"*Oui*, it sounds like something I must experience. And I may need a guide, someone to direct me to the best place to stack, eat and repeat. Would you have supper with me?"

"Oh, well, I'd...."

He waited for an excuse, knowing it had been a gamble, but when she started to nod and then enthusiastically declared, "Why not!" his heart did a little flip.

The sound of the helicopter's rotating blades chopped the air. "Perfect timing. Tell me where the best buffet is and I will have our pilot drop us close."

Cady hefted her pack over a shoulder. "I'm not sure there are any hotels in Vegas that have helipads anymore. But I can get us close. Are you sure you want to experience American cuisine at its fastest and most certainly furious?"

"I do!"

CHAPTER THREE

After a round through the neon-lit buffet, Sabre's plate was heaped, spilling garlic-glazed shrimp and butterscotch pudding and dark gravy onto the table. Cady leaned forward, inspecting the various foods.

"I think you've managed to get at least one of everything they have to offer. That's quite the feat!"

"I do enjoy the challenge! But, Cady, how will you maintain your gorgeous figure if you do not eat?" He gestured to her plate, which was half-filled with lean chicken, salad, grapes and cantaloupe. "Is this not the place where we stack, eat and repeat? You did not go for it."

She laughed and tucked a napkin across her lap. "You have fun with it. I'm still satisfied from that protein bar."

He shook his head. "Women. Why is it you all feel you mustn't eat what you desire? I would like to see you make yourself happy by eating whatever it is that appeals to you."

"I am happy. I like chicken." And avoiding greasy foods and sweets was the only way to maintain a weight she would never be pleased with but had settled, years ago, on accepting.

"Very well." Sabre plucked a curl of shrimp from the top of his heap and tossed it in the air, catching it smartly in his mouth. With a boyish grin, he picked up his fork and dove into his stack. "I always like to indulge in the local cuisine, no matter where I visit."

"Fast food is local to the United States. But so is heart disease and obesity."

"I keep active. No worries there."

Indeed. The man was a work of art, physically. Beyond the handsome face and chiseled jawline, he sported muscles beneath the thin black sweater that molded to his body. And those loose cargo pants that he'd stuffed his gear in earlier did not hide his sexy swagger. A tamed panther. The man was possessed of utter confidence in every movement he made, be it serious photography to silly eating. And it was outrageously sexy.

The thought to send Lynn a thank-you card for coming down with a cold occurred to her. Maybe? Too much? At the very least, the day had sparked her appetite for more travel. Like *real* travel. Out of the state, even. And, as she'd mentioned to Sabre, she may even consider booking a flight.

But small steps, Cady. Take it easy!

On the other hand, she could talk herself out of a vacation *like that.* How to blossom this new feeling of impending adventure? It felt so imminent and like if she didn't jump now, she might never make that leap.

"So." Following a bite of mashed potatoes, Sabre forked in a wobble of red gelatin. "I will allow the light eating, but now you must tell me something."

"Okay?"

"All day you continually assured me you were there to make me happy. To make sure I had whatever it was I needed. And you did. *Merci.* But—" Now he leaned over his heaped plate and with a lift of one brow, asked conspiratorially, "I want to know what makes *you* happy."

"Me?" She teased at her salad sans dressing with the fork. The answer came by rote. "I like seeing others happy." Which meant life was just easier when the boat didn't rock from sudden waves of discontent surrounding her.

Sabre made a scoffing noise. Something he'd done a few times in the desert and she'd decided was a French thing. "No, no, Cady. We are focusing on you right now." He again leaned across his plate and said, "If a person existed… Let's say, just like you, who lives to make others happy, how would that person make *you* happy?"

How, indeed? "I don't know." Did they really

have to play this game? Who cared about Cady Burton's happiness? The question felt so alien. It set her spine straight and made her clasp her fork tighter. "It's not part of my job—"

"Uh-uh. We have agreed that you are off the clock now. So, talk to me, *oui*? I'd like to get to know you better. You appeal to me."

Cady felt a healthy blush rise and took a sip of water. When was the last time a man had been so genuinely interested in her without expecting something in return, like sex? Not that she was against sex; she just preferred it to take its time, happen naturally.

Why was she thinking about sex? Oh, right. Sex-on-a-stick sitting across the table from her.

"Let's start easy," Sabre said. He settled back and as he spoke, forked in bites from the mini smorgasbord before him. "What snacks would this person who provides happiness pack for you?"

"That's easy. Gummy bears and lemon-flavored spring water."

"Ah? You like the squishy little bears?"

"Especially the red ones."

"I will remember that." If a wink were capable of foreplay, the man had mastered the sensuous move. Cady could feel her spine loosen as if a taut string had released. "And where would the Conductor of Happiness book a room for you in Las Vegas?"

"Oh, I don't need a place fancy. Any hotel is fine."

"Cady."

The way he said her name—*Kay Dee*—with equal emphasis on each of the two syllables did something dangerous to her inhibitions.

Sabre pushed his plate aside and put his hands on the table between them. She was intensely aware of how masculine they were, how she might like to experience his fingers tracing her skin. Capturing her essence in a very different manner than he had on film. "This is a fantasy, your dreams and desires. What makes you happy. So, tell me."

A fantasy, eh? If only he could read her mind!

"Okay, then… I'd want to stay at the Paris hotel, because I'd like to visit Paris someday. Taste all the French cuisine and climb to the top of the Eiffel Tower."

"Ah? My home base. I think you would enjoy the City of Lights. It offers many wonders beyond the usual tourist traps."

"Well, if I ever did visit, I'd have to do the tourist traps. Those are the things I've seen in pictures and are what make up my dreams."

"Fair enough. I can admit the Eiffel Tower is impressive. We are close neighbors, the Iron Lady and I. She peeks into my bedroom all the time."

There was that sexy wink again. Cady almost choked on a chunk of cantaloupe. Another sip of water saved her from that embarrassment. Did the man realize the power he had over her with a mere wink? She had dated some handsome men, but none so casually sensual, and possessed of an almost supernatural talent at flirtation.

Cady, relax! Don't act as dorky as your sweater makes you look!

"Have you lived in Paris all your life?"

"I have. Our family traces its genealogy back three centuries. We own land south of Paris, and many properties in the city. We are—rumored, of course, my brother is currently having our genealogy confirmed—supposed to be direct descendants of Henri d'Aramitz. Do you know who that is?"

"I don't. Sorry."

"Have you read *The Three Musketeers*?"

"Of course! I love a good swashbuckler story. Adventure in a foreign country? I'm so there."

"Well, then you know Henri d'Aramitz. Dumas based the character of Aramis on the real man, who was a chevalier. And he was related to the real-life person whom Dumas used to create the character of Porthos. All Dumas's musketeers were crafted from real people, including D'Artagnan!"

"I didn't know that. So your ancestor was a musketeer? That's so cool!"

He shrugged. "I used to play swashbuckler with

my *grand-père*'s épée when I was a kid. I dashed my sword at anything that would fight back, including the old tin weathervane that had been placed on a fence post hugging the forest behind our Rhône château."

"Such childhood adventuring must have fueled your desire to travel the world with your camera," Cady decided.

"It did." He studied his plate, touching a bit of dripping gravy, then shook his head. "You are right about too much food. I need some good wine to cap this off. Do you want to go to a quiet lounge?"

"Quiet? Probably not in Vegas. But we could head to the Bellagio, which is close." She checked her watch. It was 10:00 p.m. "You know your direct flight to Oulu leaves early in the morning."

"*Oui*. Where am I staying tonight, by the way?"

"At the Bellagio," she said. "Sorry, I should have made sure you had your itinerary. The day got away from me when it took a weird turn this morning. I'm usually much more organized. I apologize—"

His touch to the back of her hand arrested her apology with a gasp. And when he clasped her hand, she looked up into his eyes. The sputtering candle on the table flickered, making his irises sparkle with whimsy.

"Stop apologizing, Cady. You do not exist to make me happy. I can take care of that myself."

"It is my job to—sorry." She winced. "I know I'm off the clock, and I will stop apologizing. Maybe? It's so ingrained. I'm—" She bit her lower lip.

Nervous? Hell yes! Unaccustomed to being wined and dined—albeit at a food trough—by a handsome Frenchman? Mercy. And now she had suggested it was a good idea that he head off to his room? What was she doing? She didn't want this night to end.

"I think a drink is necessary." Sabre stood and offered her a crooked arm. "I promise I won't keep you out late. But do indulge me one cocktail?"

"Of course," she allowed herself to say. Because making people happy was not an easy habit to drop.

But really? There was no way she could refuse Sabre d'Aramitz anything he should ask. She had followed him across a desert. And a part of her very soul had opened up to the wonder that he was a master at capturing. Now to see what other wonders he might offer her.

Sabre could see Cady figuratively prodding at the protective shell she wore about herself. Yes, she wore some figurative armor beneath that sweater. He hadn't suggested they have a drink because he wanted to loosen her up and—well, no, he hadn't lascivious intentions in mind. He had simply needed a glass of wine to erase the lingering tastes of the buffet food. It left a certain *something* on his palate.

But he had not wanted the night to end as well. Not so quickly. So he'd followed that urge for more, and now here he sat, in utter pleasure, nursing a martini and listening to his muse talk. But his oft-spurned heart did silently warn not to make this anything more than just a few drinks.

As they chatted by the bar, he teased out from Cady how she had lived in Vegas all her life and enjoyed taking on tasks that required order. Sabre realized she *lived* for order. Chaos was likely not a word that even entered her vocabulary. Complete opposite of him. Which was probably why she was constantly apologizing for not making things perfect for him. He was a big boy; he could take care of his needs just fine. And besides, perfection was boring.

However, the more he listened to her talk, and watched her mouth form words—those beautiful, lush pink lips that a man could indulge in with a kiss—the more he wanted to lean in and kiss her. But the moment felt off. Not in a crowded bar. He didn't want to share such an intimate moment with the crowd.

She'd checked her watch. Again. She probably

didn't stay out late, yet felt she was obligated to entertain a client. Perhaps he was simply a freelance hire to her. He shouldn't entertain it being anything more between them. Him and women? It always tended to start out so well, then abruptly fall off the proverbial cliff. He'd yet to find the one woman who could keep up with him and fit into his life. So he'd stopped looking.

And yet… Cady was the first woman who held him absolutely entranced while talking about mundane things such as filing client reports and organizing the company's holiday party. Didn't matter what she talked about. He liked being near her, hearing the melodious tones of her soft voice, feeling the warmth of her presence. Inhaling her fresh fruit scent. And her hair was like fire. A fire upon which he wanted to burn himself.

"Sabre?"

"Huh?"

She blinked at him. "The bartender wants to know if you'd like another."

"Oh… Uh…" He gestured *no* and the bartender moved on to the next customer. "Sorry, I was captivated."

Cady looked over her shoulder and around the vast bar, which was hugged by poker tables and high rollers yelling for big money and luck beneath a canopy of flashing neon.

He couldn't understand how she could be so

unaware of her beauty. French women owned their beauty, be it drop-dead or simple, or even oddly imperfect.

Sabre stroked the back of Cady's hand. "I am captivated by *you*," he said. "Only by you."

"You're quite the charmer, Monsieur d'Aramitz."

"You are okay with my charm? Remember, you are not on the job right now."

"Yes, I am okay with it. You make me forget to…"

To think only of others, he silently filled in for her.

"But I do think I should head home." She gathered her purse and slipped the strap over a shoulder. "It's nearing midnight. I have to be at work in the morning. And you have an early flight."

"I'm so sorry. Yes, I will let you go. I guess I cannot walk you to your door because I am staying here."

"The valet will bring my car around. I believe the driver will escort you to Victory Marketing in the morning to meet up with Lynn before the two of you head to the airport. So… I'll see you again in the morning?"

So that was it? See you later, au revoir? Obviously, she wasn't the slightest bit interested in him beyond making him happy for her job. That clawed at Sabre's heart in a surprising way. It wasn't as though he was looking for a commitment from Cady. All he wanted was…a few more minutes. To bask in her presence so he could recall it later when he needed a smile.

"I, uh…" She slid off the barstool before him and touched his forearm. "I had a really good time with you today, Sabre. It was fun. Being with you made me happy."

"Then that makes me happy. Because I sense Cady's happiness is not an easy thing."

She smirked. "Probably not. But take some credit in knowing you've sparked my desire to consider traveling."

"I will." As she started to turn away, Sabre reacted. *Grand-père*'s voice said he mustn't miss any chance at grasping all the world offered. "Let me walk you out."

Her green eyes glittered with spotlights from the surrounding lights, and she nodded. Sabre's heart pinged like the distant slot machines.

He took her hand and, when he felt no resistance—that was a good sign—he led her down the carpeted hallway and turned sharply down a narrow aisle and past a sign that advertised that the last show had closed, please return tomorrow at the designated time.

Coming to a stop, Sabre spun Cady around and she settled with her back against the wall.

"I want to kiss you," he said. Because—screw it—he didn't want to regret *not* saying as much.

A tug at her lower lip with her teeth teased at him. The sparkle in her green eyes said things the astute secretary might not dare put into words. Her lush lashes drew his attention. To feel them flutter against his cheek, and then as a whisper against his mouth?

But he could read that quiet invitation. So she did have a daring side to her. One that went beyond helicopter rides and desert hikes. Sabre put his hands over her shoulders and hugged her against the wall. His compulsion was to kiss her quickly, without another ask for permission, because he didn't want her to overthink the moment, to second-guess her rash decision.

He slid a hand down to her hip and eased his body against her lush curves. Her crazy curves ramped up his desires. Yet, he felt her palms push gently against his chest, he pulled away from the imminent kiss and—with matching chuckles, they both noted her sweater was flashing.

Cady laughed gaily. "Oh, dear, I guess you really know how to—"

"Turn you on?" he suggested.

He wanted to invite her up to his room where their kiss could be private. And he didn't. Too quick. Too greedy. But then, that was it, wasn't it? He'd see her briefly in the morning, and then not ever again? He didn't want it to end so quickly like this. Something about her felt…different. Worth exploring.

So he leaned in again. A couple of men in suits walked past them, talking loudly about the blonde at the bar. They paused at the end of the hall to light up cigarettes. They weren't going anywhere.

And Sabre wasn't about to kiss the woman with an audience. Kiss fail. He shook his head and smiled at Cady. She touched her mouth and shook her head. That was Sabre's cue to end this. For now. He couldn't fathom not seeing her again, spending more time with her, learning her.

Kissing her.

"Will you give me your number so I can text you?" he asked. "I want to keep in touch. You never know when I'll be in Vegas on a shoot." He scrolled to Contacts in his phone and handed it to her. "Take my info as well. If you would?"

"I'd like that very much. I wish you were staying longer."

"Are you saying that because you still want to see if I can finish a full plate of buffet food?" he teased.

With a laugh, and a glance to the smoking gentlemen, she handed him back his phone. "You guessed it. I'll get your contact info from my file at work."

He took her hand and kissed it, then held it

against his cheek. The closest he would get to kissing her mouth. “Au revoir, Cady.”

And before she could reply, he walked away. Because really, he wasn’t the romantic sort. And he knew if he stood before her any longer, with his body brushing against her hard nipples, he’d find some way to get her to his room. And then? Well, then he’d regret it. Because Cady was not that kind of woman. And he was glad of that.

But while his heart protested this curt parting, it was also a familiar feeling he had learned to embrace. That of loneliness. And Sabre d’Aramitz was a master at being alone.

CHAPTER FOUR

CADY BREEZED INTO Victory Marketing and went through her getting-ready routine in record time. The world was bright. Her heart felt light.

Seating herself at command central and leaning back to survey the upper offices through the glass partitions on each of the floors, she suddenly felt…like there was more. So much more than keeping an office organized and her life moving on a straight and even path.

And she knew what that *more* entailed.

That *more* looked very much like Sabre d'Aramitz's life. He was free to go where he wished when he wished. Travel the world. See all the amazing sights it offered. Learn new things. Talk to people from different cultures. Answer to no one but himself. And do it all with a sexy smile and a wink.

Sabre had inspired her to look beyond her normal routine. To actually peel the cobwebs off her dreams of seeing the world and begin to figure out how to make it happen. Maybe?

Take it slow, Cady. You are not a jumper, but rather a wader.

Right. But it didn't hurt to start that wade with some serious planning. She had a little in savings. Enough for a flight and perhaps a week in an overseas location. It wasn't as if she were saving for something she needed, like a car repair or new heater—though she did keep an emergency fund just for such a purpose. Dare she hop on an airplane and venture out of her comfort zone?

"Someday," she whispered.

Whew! A mere day spent with Monsieur d'Aramitz had turned her world upside down. The man had gotten under her skin. Inspirationally, and…in a good, sexy, want-to-see-you-again-and-again way.

Cady's shoulders dropped. Alas, after this morning she would never see him again.

Should she have been more aggressive last night? Suggested they go up to his room to experience that imminent kiss that had been rudely stopped by those men? Who could remain in a romantic mood around a cloud of disgusting cigarette smoke?

Cady sighed. It had only been a missed kiss, not a wild night of delicious sex with a Frenchman.

While it had been almost a year since her last boyfriend—they'd broken up on Valentine's Day of all days—she wasn't desperate for sex. And had she gone up to Sabre's room, she would have gone into that liaison knowing she'd not see him again. A one-night stand was not her style. Not even for the delicious memory of having slept with him. She preferred to date a man, getting to know him better, before shedding any articles of clothing.

And yet…

She jiggled the computer mouse and the screen awakened to the last page she'd had open, which was an article on Sabre. His smile teased her with a wicked curve. Light brown eyes, like whiskey on ice, twinkled with adventurous tales untold. And kisses not given. *Argh!*

He'd held her against the wall, not roughly, but firmly. She'd never kissed a man whose confidence oozed like a natural pheromone. The moment hadn't felt naughty, or wrong. It had been a new adventure, a dare her heart had secretly challenged her to accept. Like belting herself inside a helicopter and soaring over the Nevada desert.

Yet, that missed kiss had been the end of it. Cady must resign herself that she'd had a wonderful time with an interesting and intriguing man. And those were memories to cherish.

"You're too careful," she muttered, the word her mother so often used to label her daughter. Always so concerned that she wouldn't fall into the ways of her mother. Random men picked up in casinos, bodacious flirtations that led to the morning walk of shame. More than a few times Cady had received a call from Maria Burton, asking her to pick her up from a hotel because she didn't have cab fare. A constant reminder that if Cady were not careful, she might end up in the same position.

Not even that, though. Cady was simply afraid she couldn't control things if she loosened up and just let life roll toward her, permeate her being and have its way with her.

Life having its way with her? Silly. But Sabre d'Aramitz having his way with her? A one-night stand wouldn't have killed her. It wouldn't mark her as a shameless woman deserving of a big red letter on her shirt. She was a grown woman; she could do whatever she wanted behind closed doors.

Alas, daydreams were called fantasies for a reason.

She pulled up the flight information for Lynn and Sabre's leg to the Oulu airport in Finland and verified the details. And as she did, the front door swung open and in walked a fantasy she'd regretfully decided to shelve.

Clad in the same sporty khakis, canvas jacket and leather gloves, Sabre strode toward her, a hero gliding toward destiny on the movie screen. "Bonjour, Cady!"

"Mercy," Cady whispered. A flutter inside her rib cage made her sigh.

Maybe she could pull that fantasy out a little bit? Preen over the cover and read a few more pages before it left for another shelf?

She stood and tugged down her skirt. No silly holiday sweater today. Knowing she'd see Sabre, she had chosen a soft teal sweater dress and a long crystal necklace that dangled to her stomach. Hair perfectly styled and extra fluffed? Check. Nails freshly polished and lipstick the same shade as her polish? Check. A spritz of her favorite perfume. Double check.

"Monsieur d'Aramitz." Then she regretted the formal greeting. They had almost kissed! "I mean… Sabre."

Would he want to give it another try? They were alone.

In the office. Definitely a no-go for her.

She walked around the desk to greet him with a handshake, but he tugged her to him—and just when she expected a kiss, he instead hugged her. Generously. Warmly. And with a sigh she felt vibrate through her entire body.

With one eye veering toward the front door to ensure no one from work entered, Cady wondered if the hug would turn into a kiss. Yes! *No, not here*. Her stomach whirled and butterflies spun up to her throat and pulsed throughout her system.

"Apples," he whispered before pulling back from their embrace. "I was hoping I'd have opportunity to inhale that delicious scent again. You smell like a pie, Cady."

"Oh, dear. I'm not sure that's the effect I am going for with my perfume."

"I love it. Every time I eat apple pie, I will think of you."

"Oh?"

He would think of her.

Because he would not see her again. Darn, she should have let her hair down last night! At the very least, kissed him now. Was she bold enough to try it? Probably his hug meant kisses were off the table.

Right, Cady. This is work. Not some wild daydream come to life.

"Did you bring in your bags?" she asked.

"I had the driver take them to the airport. He'll check them in for me. I could have met your liaison there as well, but I had to come see you again, Cady. I wish it were you who was flying across the ocean with me today."

Her ears warmed. "Is that really something you'd wish for after seeing how terribly I suffered the helicopter ride?" She hadn't gotten sick, but had needed a few moments to herself behind the way station to gather her wits and realize she was still in one piece and hadn't crash-landed.

"It was your first flight! And you weathered it rather well. Flying will be a breeze for you now. I promise."

"If you say so. I've actually begun thinking about where I might vacation someday. I've never been on one because of my fear of flying."

"Then I have inspired you to take the leap? That pleases me." His words sounded like something he would say in bed, lying naked next to her, his kisses dotting her skin.

"I aim to please," she said on a breathy note. Then, at the sight of the front door opening, she straightened. "Oh, there's Lynn."

Heart dropping, because their time alone had been cut short, and she really wanted to know all the many ways to please him beyond flying, Cady stepped aside Sabre so their distance was more friendly and less intimate. "Lynn…" her coworker wobbled toward them "…are you okay?"

"Fine," she whispered. At the sight of Sabre, Lynn straightened, winced, then forced a smile. The tiny blonde who normally zinged through the office with a cup of high-octane coffee in one hand and her eyes glued to her phone in the other, looked a shell of herself.

"Lynn." Cady approached her and took her

hand. Clammy. Was that a bead of sweat at her temple? "I've got everything packed for you. This is Sabre d'Aramitz. Sabre, this is Lynn Marshall, our client liaison."

Lynn offered a shaky hand to Sabre, which he reluctantly shook. No bussing of the cheeks? Wise man.

"Just coming off a miserable flu," Lynn rasped. "I'll rally on the flight to Finland. I'm so pleased to meet you, Monsieur d'Aramitz."

"Likewise. Uh…" Sabre glanced to Cady.

His look screamed for something: understanding, help, a confirmation that he was not the only one who had determined the woman who was about to spend eight hours in a tin can with him was still sick and likely contagious.

Sabre tugged at his jacket. "Madame Marshall, I suspect you are not well enough to fly, *oui*?"

"Oh, don't worry." Lynn winced. "Just…a little wobbly. Once I board the plane, I'll down some cold medicine and sleep it off. I don't want to let you down, monsieur."

"I see. Well, uh…"

Sabre looked to Cady. And in his eyes, she saw a glint. And the corner of his mouth began a smile. What was he thinking?

"I appreciate your dedication to the job," he said to Lynn. "Victory Marketing has always been very good to me. In your absence Mademoiselle

Burton represented Victory above and beyond. And...uh...it would be a disappointment if Mademoiselle Burton was not allowed to accompany me on the second leg of the assignment."

Lynn flashed a look to Cady. Even in her wearied state, her gaze bubbled with hope. If she'd suspected she couldn't have made this leg of the trip, she could have called in again instead of suffering her way into the office.

"We've developed a rapport," Sabre continued. "Mademoiselle Burton knows how I work and is an excellent assistant. I had considered asking you to trade places with her again, and now... seeing your condition..."

"I'm really just...fine..." Lynn gasped. "But if you insist..."

Sabre rushed to catch a palm against her shoulder. And as he did, Lynn went down in a faint. He swung around, grabbing her across the torso so she didn't hit the floor, and gently lowered her to lay on the shiny marble surface. He adjusted her hair away from her face—a caring action—then stood over her. Hands to his hips, he looked to Cady, utterly aghast.

"I'll call her boyfriend." Cady veered around the desk. "She needs to be home in bed."

"I would say so." Sabre stood over the fallen woman, scratching the back of his head. "Valliant, though, wouldn't you say?"

"Yes, she's certainly a trooper. But I'd step back if I were you. You don't want to catch whatever has taken her out."

"Good call." He took two big steps backward.

Half an hour later, after Lynn had been revived and her boyfriend arrived to scoot her back home and into bed, the woman agreed that Cady should take her place again. And she'd whispered to Cady as she'd handed her the water bottle, "Bless you, Cady. Do good by Victory Marketing, for me, okay?"

"You can rely on me."

Cady turned to the sexy Frenchman who stood at the door, his hand held out for her to take. The limo sat waiting out by the curb. "Ready?" he asked.

Why did it suddenly disturb her to think that she was going to fly across the ocean with a wealthy man and spend the next few days with him? Alone. For work. But it couldn't be work all the time. When he wasn't taking photographs of the aurora borealis, what would they do then? Would he want to spend time with her? Try for that kiss again? Sleep with her?

She shouldn't think too far into it. It was an innocent venture. For work. Nothing would come of it. And she didn't want anything to come of it.

Maybe.

Heck, you know you want something *to come of it. A fling.*

At the very least, a chance to step away from Reliable Cady and just lose herself in the joy of a new adventure.

No. This was happening too fast. She'd intended to think about travel for weeks, months, perhaps even years. Sure, she had a passport. It was a necessity for identity at work. Despite the allure of a sexy traveling companion, could she really do this?

"Cady?" Sabre prompted.

"Right." She grabbed her purse and the duffel she'd packed for Lynn. *Now or never, Cady. Make a choice to remain in your perfectly controlled life, or to take a leap.* "I'm all in."

The flight was—surprisingly—uneventful. Long. But, after the initial tense waiting for takeoff and clutching the armrests for dear life, Cady had noticed that Sabre's smile softened her fears. After the initial adjustment to the changing altitude—her ears had crackled; her skin felt itchy—she settled into the seat. This was a huge moment in her life! And with Sabre as her guide, she'd succeed in mastering the challenge.

Perhaps noticing her nervousness, he'd laughed softly and told her about his many adventures flying. First class, flight attendants flirting with him—both sexes—enduring crying babies for hours and the utter joy of a night flight snuggled in a blanket next to a fellow traveler who smelled like the spices from the country he'd just left.

After a few hours, snacks were served and Sabre had drifted to sleep. Cady took the hint and, deciding she'd seen enough clouds, figured it would be wise to, at the very least, catch a nap. She wasn't familiar with how jet lag worked, so would follow a master traveler. She slept well. Sabre gently nudged her awake as they taxied onto the landing strip in Oulu. A limo had waited to drive them the hour and a half to the port city of Kemi.

First assessment of her big adventure? A little woozy from her sleep, but the brisk winter air quickly revived that waning energy. Still, she needed a hot shower and some hair fix-it. *STAT.* As well, Cady was thankful when Sabre directed the driver to stop at a local clothing shop before heading on to the resort. Still in her sweater dress and ankle boots, she was in desperate need of clothing, especially for the extreme weather change. It was freaking cold outside!

In the shop, her love for shopping had kicked in as Sabre helped her select some winter gear, jacket, cap and gloves, boots and also some jeans and a swimsuit. The resort offered soaking spas so the suit had been a necessity. She'd charged it on her credit card. This trip would be on Victory's dime, but she did not expect them to pay for her clothing.

It was a beautiful January morning. The air was chilly and the sky a crisp blue as they drove through a gorgeous landscape to the resort. Cady couldn't even feel embarrassed that a super-sexy man sat next to her in the back seat of the limo, likely fully aware of her messy hair and growling stomach. It was exciting to see all the signs and businesses in a different language. She was in a different country! And a completely different climate.

"Look at all the snow," she remarked with awe.

"Have you never seen snow before?"

"Only on the mountains from a distance. I've never been out of Vegas. I even missed the ski trip to Colorado in high school."

Not exactly missed it. More like, hadn't had the money to fund it, and...her mom had just gotten married, if Cady remembered correctly, and all her focus had been on her new hubby, not her daughter's nonexistent social life and screaming need for friends.

"Then this must be very exciting for you."

"It is. Snow is so pretty. It sparkles like diamonds. Everything is just so white! But it is much colder than I'd expected."

Since that first step off the airplane when the wind had hit her like a razor to the cheek, she'd sucked in a cold gasp and it had settled in her stomach, forming an ice cube. But she wouldn't complain. This was a dream trip!

Happy and surprisingly contented, Cady settled back and met Sabre's gaze. That whiskey warmth beamed at her. His eyes were so expressive. She felt safe with him. Accepted. He must possess some inner alchemical skills she was not aware of.

"The aurora is only viewable at night," he said, "so we will have to find a way to fill the days."

He'd said *we*. As in the both of them. Which she appreciated. Because she was a single woman in a foreign country. All alone. She had mastered the flight. But experiencing a new country was something she preferred to do with a companion. She may be in control behind the reception desk, but this was a new frontier. And she wasn't sure how best to navigate. The adventure was on! But if she didn't take it slowly, she might crash before being able to enjoy any of it. So, she reverted to what she did best.

"I'm here to assist you in any way you should require," she offered. "I'll be ready to go when you venture out with your camera. If you wish me to accompany you at other times, I can certainly do that, too."

Sabre smirked. He took her hand. The sudden heat of his touch shocked her system with a shiver that tingled from her scalp to her toes. Who needed gloves when the man was like a portable warming station?

"You are apprehensive?" he asked.

Yes! No. Of course, she was! But she could pull on a brave face and be a good representative for Victory Marketing. That's what she did. Made others *believe* she was happy.

"You are," he decided. "I understand. When I first started traveling alone as a teenager it was daunting. Visiting places that didn't speak my language. Meeting new people and stepping into diverse cultures. Don't worry. Finland is very friendly and easy to assimilate. The Nordic esthetic is cozy and kind. They speak English, as you experienced in the clothing shop, as much as Finnish and even Swedish. And I will be by your side to guide you."

"Pretty sure that was supposed to be my job."

"We can look after one another, *oui*?"

"Works for me. But I don't want to cramp your style."

"What does that mean?"

"It means if you have plans or things to do when you are not working, I don't want to be in the way or keep you from doing them."

"Ah. When I am not snapping photos for the job, I generally like to relax and take in what the venue has to offer. And since we've both had some sleep, I suspect the jet lag will not affect you too much. How about we spend the afternoon in one of the hot spas before we trek out in search of the northern lights?"

That sounded like a dream she wasn't worthy of experiencing. But just as Cady had the thought, she chastened her inner child who was quick to pull her back from anything that would give her pleasure. Indeed, she was here to do a job, but that job could only be done at night. So, her days should be enjoyed. And she did require a segue from the long flight—a spa could easily replace a hot shower—something to restore her tightened nerves to normal.

"I'll race you to the hot tub," she said, surprising herself with her sudden abandon.

Sabre laughed and gave her hand a squeeze. "I like you, Cady. There is a woman inside that luscious body who wants to run free and discover the world. I'll uncover your hidden adventurer before this trip is over."

"You think so?"

"It will happen, Cady. Put your trust in me."

And without thinking, she conceded. "I will."

CHAPTER FIVE

THE RESORT FEATURED glass-domed igloos for their guests to lie in bed at night and view the aurora borealis. The only private glassless section of the igloos was a small attached bathroom. Victory Marketing had booked the elite room for him, which featured a king-size bed, a private hot tub and on-call room service. Obviously, something Cady had seen to. Sabre was accustomed to top-of-the-line service at his stays. But he wasn't beyond sleeping in a makeshift canvas tent in the Sahara, or even a hammock secured with pitons to the side of a cliff. A guy could go soft if he expected the world to cater to him simply because his wallet was fat.

Sure, he had hit the billion mark last year thanks to his investments. But he used that excess to enhance his life, not prove to others how much money he had. When a man couldn't even quantify his worth in a tangible way, he just had to let it ride over him.

Since Cady had missed the dinner service on the flight—he'd woken after a three-hour nap—Sabre ordered a four-course meal to be delivered to the hot tub. It would arrive within the hour. Excellent.

Cady's igloo was down a heated pathway at the edge of a small village of glass igloos, all facing north for perfect night viewing of the borealis. *If* the colored lights made an appearance. They were most prevalent in fall and spring, but January sightings were possible. He'd explained that when Victory had booked him, and they had insisted the client needed shots sooner rather than later.

Sabre checked an app on his phone that forecast weather and aurora borealis viewing stats. Tonight, due to clouds, the possibility of it showing was only 10 percent, with tomorrow up to 90. He'd still head out tonight to locate a good area to shoot. He may live adventurously and spur-of-the-moment, but he was always cognizant of his employer's expenses.

Which was why he charged all expenses beyond the room to his account. He'd also bought Cady's clothing. He'd asked the clerk to make the switch with the credit cards while Cady had been distracted by a display of lighted snowflake keychains. Like the proverbial kid in a candy store, she had delighted over the various winter clothing items.

Spending time with Cady altered his mood. There was something about her that was so light. Open to new things. Even if he did sense an extreme need to hold back, restrain herself from what she could do. The woman battled wanting to control things and pleasing others with wanting to burst free and take it all in, perhaps even seeing to her own needs.

But as he'd told her, that would change. He couldn't babysit a woman afraid to take chances. Even if she worked for his employer. He had no time for such nonsense. So far? She'd stepped up.

But could she keep up with him when it came time to strap on skis and venture out into the chilly night?

"That will be the test," he muttered.

And he knew it wasn't a necessary requirement to her job but rather a personal expectation that he shouldn't press on her but couldn't stop himself from demanding. Always, Sabre sought a woman who could keep up with him. He hadn't found one yet. Dare he hope that could someday change?

Cady was in a country she had never been to before, soaking in a hot tub surrounded by snow, of all things. How crazy was her life all of a sudden?

Many thanks to whatever bug Lynn had caught. But certainly, she did hope Lynn wasn't suffering. Too much.

Instead of carefully tiptoeing into the idea of someday traveling, she had literally been pushed into the pool. So far, she seemed to be treading water. But the challenge of absorbing the new experience alongside a man who made her better judgment wrestle with her inner wild child would prove daunting.

And she couldn't stop thinking about that almost kiss. Had it been a mistake? Did Sabre think of it as a mistake? Was he relieved it hadn't happened? He hadn't brought it up. Best to follow his lead.

This was work.

But not all work. Cady blew out a breath. Her ability to float as she tread the waters could grow weaker if she were not careful. Like right now. Sitting in a hot tub? Definitely not work. The brisk walk from her igloo to slip into the tub had prickled her skin. Yet when she'd sunk into the hot water, her muscles had sighed. *Just enjoy*, her conscience reminded. And she couldn't even be bothered by the fact she wasn't a size eight.

Very well, it did make her self-conscious when she was around men. *Voluptuous* was the term she tried on, but often failed to fit into. Pleasantly plump worked for her. All her parts were snugly tucked into the one-piece suit. And she had placed a towel behind her, near her head, for a strategic swish of the towel when it came time to exit.

At the sight of the man walking toward her, Cady's breath sighed out in a cloud before her. If Sabre had appeared like a runway model to her clad in his desert khakis, now the man had taken a step up to some sort of god.

"Bonjour," he said as he stopped beside the tub. He wore sunglasses against the not-too-bright sun and black boxer shorts–style trunks.

"Bonjour," Cady said on a gasp.

Could a man look more perfect? His skin was tanned and the dark hair on his chest, legs and arms only enhanced his sex appeal. And not a shred of unnecessary fat on that man's body. Cady's eye arrowed toward his six-pack abs. As he inhaled, stretching an arm back and over his shoulder, it further enhanced those iron abs.

He slid into the tub. Not across from her, but about a two-foot distance away. "You are all right, Cady? You seem somewhat…distracted?"

"Yes. *Oui.* I mean, no, I'm not distracted." Certainly not by iron abs. "I'm just overwhelmed by—" him! "—the beauty of Finland. And I'm wearing a swimsuit, sitting in a pool, while there's snow just right there!"

Sabre gestured his hand through the steam that rose from the tub. "It's a kick, eh?"

"Absolutely. But I might never get out. It'll feel so cold out of the water."

"It will, but that's the invigorating part. There's a hot/cold sauna on the east side of the resort. Sit in the sauna until you are dripping with sweat, then dive into a cold tub, then back to the sauna, then back to the cold. You must try it."

"Is that what gives you all the muscles? Because I'll try anything for a little definition."

Sabre laughed. "It could be? I sensed you were hungry in the limo so I ordered some food for us to be delivered here."

Had he heard her stomach growl? Oh, mercy. If it wasn't a silly sweater, it was loud body noises.

"Starving," she finally admitted.

"Then you will feast on all four courses. You see? I am taking care of you as you are looking after me."

"I have a feeling our mutual monitoring will tip heavily in my favor."

He made a *pfft* sound that she'd learned was dismissive in a fun manner. "I expect nothing from you. I don't need a handler, but I know many agencies I work with require it to keep track of expenses and ensure I don't get lost. Which is very possible! And you did well in Las Vegas. Your notes are excellent. So detailed and neat. I appreciate that."

"Thank you." Appreciation always sent a skitter

of delight over the tops of her ears and down the back of her scalp. It's what she thrived on. "So, will I be skiing and note-taking tonight?"

"Not simultaneously. Unless you want to give it a go?"

Now it was Cady's turn to laugh. "Let's take it a step at a time. I had signed up Lynn for a ski class in a couple hours so I'll take her spot. Figured I'd better learn the basics."

"You impress me, Cady Burton. You take control of the situation. Even those that are quite out of your realm of experience."

"It's my superpower. Keeping things in order and making people happy. I am a people pleaser, and darn good at it."

"That you are. My superpower is jumping into the unknown."

"I get that about you. Have you always been so adventurous?"

"If you include jumping from rooftops to trampolines and racing my dirt bike through the junkyards?"

"Ah, yes, the wild child." That's where that brilliant spark in his eyes had originated. It was a mix of boyish adventure and adult charm. "You mentioned you had siblings?"

"*Oui*, a younger and older brother."

"The middle child. That makes sense."

"How so?"

"The middle child is the one who seeks the attention."

Sabre bowed his head. Cady felt his entire mood had just altered in the set of his shoulders and the lean of his body away from her. "Did I say something wrong? I'm sorry, I shouldn't get so personal—"

"No, please, you said nothing wrong. In fact, you hit me right on the head, so to speak. I have always sought attention." He shrugged. "My mother died when I was five."

"Oh, I'm so sorry."

"*Merci.* I wasn't emotionally mature enough at the time to understand that loss. But following her death, my father showered all his attention on his youngest son, who was a baby at the time. And our oldest brother knows when and how to get what he wants. Which left me standing in the middle, wondering why no one ever paid me any mind. The attention I did get was always from my *grand-père*."

Who, Cady recalled from their conversation in the desert, had died six months previously. Poor Sabre. Losing the one person who had given him attention must have really hit him hard. And he'd lost his mother, too? She could relate to the one-parent household. And the quest for attention. Cady was so accustomed to survival that when she did get positive notice from her mother, it felt like a treat. One that she must be cautious with, should it be whipped away from her reach as quickly as she reached out for it.

"Do you have siblings?" he asked.

She shook her head. "It was just me and my mother. My dad died when I was four."

"I'm sorry."

She spread her palms across the water surface and tilted her head against the edge. "Don't be. We have experienced similar losses. We were too young. And like you said, didn't know how to understand such a loss at the time. I'm a survivor," she added. "And I didn't remain fatherless for long. Well. I would never call the three husbands that my mom married over the years father material."

"Your mother has been married…four times?"

"Currently in the process of divorcing number four. I worry about her. She moved into his house. She owns very little. So, if the divorce doesn't go well, she'll be on her own with no current job to support herself."

"Then I hope she comes out of it with her fair share. Four husbands. That is a lot of commitment."

"It is. Though *commitment* is not the correct word for it. My mother has a thing for…"

Cady sensed he moved a little closer. The water shushed against her throat. Was it getting hotter?

Steam beaded on Sabre's face. So lickable. And they were talking about her mother? Why had she started this conversation? It was very personal. Too much info too soon. And no man wanted to hear her ramble on about her inattentive mother.

"A thing for...?" Sabre prompted.

A thing for rich men. They were like candy and her mother could never get enough sweets. The woman was careless with her affections. So, it wasn't exactly commitment, but rather round two, round three and so on. Bring on the next eligible bachelor!

"It's nothing," Cady said to the billionaire whom her mother would absolutely scream about if she knew her daughter stood within seduction distance of the man. To be sharing a hot tub with him?

You've hit the motherlode, Cady!

Maria Burton would call up her favorite Elvis officiant, take out a loan and fly him directly to the Oulu airport. *STAT.*

"I shouldn't have said anything. This is work."

"No, it's not." He shifted his body so he was even closer to her. Steam rose around his face. Cady had to bite back her tongue to keep it from lashing out and licking him. "Work doesn't start until the sun sets. *Oui*?"

She wasn't sure what he was getting at. But on the other hand, she wanted to believe he was suggesting they could be…something more than business associates. Perhaps even… Might that missed kiss be on the table once again? Could a man be more breathtaking? Seriously, he had to be aware of his allure and its effect on women.

"I must confess something to you," Sabre said. He hooked an elbow on the edge of the tub and peered closely at her. "The moment I saw how terrible Madame Marshall looked this morning, I was excited. My chance to spend more time with you. So promise me one thing, Cady. That it will be nothing but pleasure when we are not photographing the aurora borealis. We have a limited time together. Let's make the most of it. Deal?"

Staring at her reflection in his sunglasses, Cady saw the woman inside her who had already peeled away the restraint of careful modesty and wanted to shimmy, shedding it to the ground. *Look at me! I've come undone!*

He'd been excited to know they could spend more time together? It was a good thing she couldn't see his eyes. Forget the shedding of restraints. She'd condense into a mist and rise into the air.

Let's make the most of it.

"Cady," he teased. "I insist you say *deal*."

Was this a deal with the devil or simply an unattainable Frenchman? Either way, she would not expect it to last beyond the next few days. How could it? Her careful exterior began to melt away and sink into the hot water. "Deal. Pleasure is…"

"For everyone," he said in a sensual purr.

She was but a bow of her head away from a kiss. Her heart thundered in anticipation. No smoking strangers leering at them nearby. Just warm bubbling water that emulated the giddy bubbling in her core. And Sabre's irresistible presence. One nudge of her nose closer…

At that moment, the food arrived on a silver cart. And Cady's heart dropped.

"Foiled by the delivery service," Sabre said with a smirk. "We are not doing so well on the kiss, eh?"

Cady could but offer him a wilting smile.

As he thanked the staff member for the food, Cady realized he was as upset over that missed kiss as she felt. Was it not meant to be?

Apparently, not.

CHAPTER SIX

CADY WAITED FOR Sabre at the entrance to a trail that guided tourists around the outskirts of the resort. Here and there, it wended into the thick forest of pine trees that hugged the property. Sabre intended to move beyond the trail. The staff knew where he was headed, and how long he intended to stay out. He carried a sat phone in his gear should he need to call for help.

"Hey!" Cady called as he neared.

His chest lifted and his backpack suddenly felt less heavy. A snow bunny in white snow pants and jacket waved at him. Topped with a bright red cap that had long ties hanging to her chest where red pom-poms bobbed. She'd already strapped into her skis, wore a backpack and, with ski poles in hand, looked ready to go.

He couldn't remember a time when he'd invited a woman along on an adventure—and she'd beat him to the starting line. But he'd hold off on congratulating her. They had a long night ahead of them. Maybe. If the app was correct, they mightn't see the aurora borealis at all. Didn't matter. He wanted to scope out the landscape and find the perfect spot for when the sky did light up.

"Want to race?" he challenged as he stopped beside her and stepped into his skis. The bindings clicked and he was set to go.

"Maybe after I've had some experience using these things. The class basically gave me confidence that I wouldn't topple over, but we'll see how long my stamina lasts." She tapped the headlamp on her cap and the bright light flashed in Sabre's face. "I figured it might be helpful tonight."

Sabre reached up and turned off the headlamp. "You see how bright the sky is right now?" The eggplant sky gave off a pale glow and sparkled on the snow-covered surface like diamonds. While not daylight, it was more like twilight. "It's not going to get much darker. But we may need that lamp if we traverse through wooded areas."

"Do you know where you're going?"

He shrugged. "Life isn't worth the trip if you always know where you're going." A tease. "Don't worry, I know how to use a compass!"

With that, he took off on the trail, leading the way. He looked back over his shoulder a few times. Cady kept up with his moderate pace. He wouldn't push her.

Yet another missed kiss! He'd almost wanted to push the food delivery cart away and send off the man earlier. Was he not meant to kiss Cady? She'd certainly looked disappointed. Which had pleased him. But who could take pleasure in the fact that they'd not kissed?

He was no man to give up on a mission. And now that they'd been granted a few more days together, well, he was inclined to see how far things could develop between them. A fling in Finland? He really did crave the physical connection. And he sensed Cady was open to, at the very least, a kiss. It was best he kept it to that, too. She would be leaving his side soon enough. And he wasn't prepared to put himself through another emotional loss.

"The air is so crisp here!" she called from behind him. And later, "I think we've gone off the trail." And after he'd navigated them across a vast smooth field that led to an outcrop of rocks, "Look at the snow! It sparkles like a million diamonds!"

No complaints so far. The woman earned points for being a trooper. And for the lush shape of her encased in that white snow gear. Truly, some kind of snow bunny.

"Let's stop here!" he called back.

Did he hear a sigh of relief? Ha!

A flat rocky surface offered the perfect place to shrug off his heavy gear and it would provide level ground to set up a tripod. In the distance, the sky was framed by massive boulders and a jut of trees silhouetted against a swath of deep forest green dashing through the deep purple sky. The Baltic Sea lay just beyond another line of trees. He liked it. But clouds muted the sky.

"Just how far do we have to go to find the aurora?" Cady clicked out of the skis, and when she settled on the rock near him, he heard her huff from exertion.

"I think we've gone far enough for tonight. You feeling okay?"

She nodded, obviously out of breath. Her cheeks were rosy, not dangerously red, so he didn't fear frostbite. Their activity would keep them warm enough.

"It's good exercise," she finally offered. "Thanks for not going so fast. I know you weren't going top speed."

"You impress me that you kept up. Your first time out on skis? Remarkable."

She suddenly let her shoulders and head fall backward and landed, arms stretched out, across the rock. "Let's see how remarkable I am when it comes time to return to the resort. I need a few minutes to…catch my breath."

"I'd suggest one of the energy pods I carry along, but one of those things might keep you awake all through the night."

"I'll stick with the electrolyte drink I brought."

She leaned up to rest on an elbow and watched as he assembled the tripod. "How much does your gear weigh?"

"About seventy pounds?"

"That's crazy. You're carrying a small child on your back."

"Well..." He thought about that one. Weird image. "I don't have a child, so there you go."

"Do you want children?"

He smirked at the personal question, but didn't mind. There was something about her that made him feel so comfortable. Like he could tell her anything. Hell, he'd never told anyone about how his *grand-père* had been the only one who'd given him the attention he'd desperately sought as a child.

"I don't know about having children," he offered. "I must marry first. And finding a woman who will travel the world with me is key to that match."

"I'm sure any number of women would travel anywhere you asked them. You're an easy follow."

Sabre chuckled. "Would you follow me anywhere?"

She bopped one of the pom-poms hanging from her cap. "Depends on how far, how fast and how hot. I don't think I'd do volcanos well. I saw the photo series you did on the Krakatoa volcano where you were lowered into one by a helicopter. You're crazy."

"That experience was awesome," he said elatedly. "But, yes, very hot. I wore a special fireproof suit and had to fireproof my equipment as well. I would never ask you to follow me into a volcano, Cady."

"Good to know. I don't get paid enough for that. You want something to munch on? I brought along some of those butter buns from dinner earlier."

He held out his hand and she handed him one. He loved the cardamom and vanilla flavors in the dense treat. He ate it while adjusting the camera lens, marking the distance and the best angle.

"What made you want to capture nature like you do?" she asked. The foil that she used to wrap the buns crinkled softly.

"I told you my *grand-père* handed down his love of photography to me. He was an award-winning nature photographer."

"Right, but did he tell you the best place to photograph a volcano was from inside?"

Sabre laughed. "No, he was more protective of me. Would text me often when he knew I was on a dangerous assignment."

Remembering those texts formed a hot spinning ball in his heart. He would miss that caring communication. How to manage without that unconditional attention?

Hell. He had to change his thinking. Grandpère would scoff at his maudlin pauses. And the last thing he wanted to do was break down in front of Cady in the middle of a vast ice and snow landscape. Their deal to make the most of this time they had together? He took that seriously. And when not working, he intended to get to know her much more intimately.

"There's so much out there to see beyond the rush of the cities and humanity," he said. "Other worlds. Unique living creatures. Entire natural landscapes so alien to our usual expectations. I feel like I'll never see it all before I die. And in the process of trying to see it all, with my photographs, I can pass along the wonder to those who might never get the opportunity to see such things firsthand."

"I love that."

Here and there, where the clouds parted, stars pinpricked the violet-black atmosphere. He snapped a few shots. Nothing remarkable. Until he veered the lens downward and focused on Cady. Her arms were spread out, totally relaxed. Each breath condensed before her lips. Eyes closed, and a smile on her face, she embodied peaceful exhilaration. And those rosy cheeks were like sensual blushes.

She popped open one eye. "Are you taking pictures of me again?"

"Guilty." Moving closer to stand above her, he continued to click away. "You're more interesting than a bunch of stars that are billions of light-years away."

She shrugged. "I don't know. I could gaze at stars all night."

"You've seen one star? You've seen them all. But you, right now? Remarkable."

She bent an arm over her face. Always so sweetly shy.

Sabre sat next to her and set down the camera near his boot. "We are all remarkable. The fact that we exist, on this treacherous planet, makes us survivors. That we can move from a dry desert heat to a chilly Nordic tundra without having our bodies protest and break down is amazing. We are the children of those stars I find so boring right now. You, Cady, are a star lying in the snow."

"And that is why they call you The Wonder Maverick." She pushed up to sit and wrapped her arms about her bent legs. "I'm thankful Lynn was sick. These last couple of days with you have given me a new perspective. I saw things in the desert that I've never noticed before, even after living there for nearly thirty years. And you made me see them. I appreciate that."

"I must say you've done the same for me." He picked up the camera and sorted through the shots he'd taken of her, showing her the screen. "I wasn't sure I'd have the courage to step out and snap shots again after my *grand-père*'s death. Still feel a little shaky whenever I think of the old man. But, look at these images. I love what I have captured on your face. A curious serenity, *oui*? I feel that wonder again."

"That's weird, because I'm not a star or the aurora borealis. I'm just a person. Plain old Cady—"

Compelled to silence her need to constantly reduce herself, Sabre leaned over and kissed her. Their mouths were cool. Noses icy. But that first connection sparked a delicious heat.

Taking his time, he learned the shape of her mouth as it further warmed and softened to conform against his. She tasted like butter and cardamom. And smelled like apples. So much he wanted to glide a hand along her curvy hip and tug her closer, but their winter gear resigned him to be happy with some padded closeness.

When she pulled him down to her, he knew he'd made the right move. The kiss deepened, teasing at a passionate fire that was frilled with the chill of their icy cheeks brushing now and then. A man never need worry about frostbite if Cady were near enough to kiss. Her deep-throated sigh grew into a soft moan. Sabre ended the kiss and studied the smile in her eyes.

"Finally," she whispered.

"I agree." The next kiss felt as if they had

known the shape of one another's mouths forever. They fit. They recognized. They settled into a perfect connection. He'd kissed her to silence her from diminishing herself. This woman was not common—she was a goddess.

"Please don't ever speak of yourself in such a reductive way around me," he said. "I don't see you as any less than remarkable."

"If you say so."

"Cady," he gently warned. "You are remarkable."

"I am..." She couldn't say the word.

It hurt him that she didn't experience that immense feeling of being a part of something so great. Something he always felt when he was out on a shoot. That feeling of being one with anything and everything in nature and the world. That feeling that he belonged, no matter what his thoughts tried to convince him when he was back in the real world.

He wasn't sure how to help her to see what he saw so easily. Certainly, he was not perfect and needed a lot of help himself to see beyond his imperfections. But he had never been a man to judge a woman by her shape, surface beauty or social media status. Intelligence and a sense of self attracted him. Cady hadn't yet tapped into her true self. But she was close.

Another kiss caressed her mouth. Noses nudged.

His heartbeat did a silly stutter that made him smile against her lips.

When she shivered and her breath hushed against his cheek, he came back to the moment. And took in the fact that if his backside was feeling the icy chill from the rock they currently sat on, then surely Cady felt it, too.

"I think we should return to the resort," he said. "The lights are not going to come out tonight. Too many clouds. But tomorrow the aurora alerts look promising. Perhaps we might take these kisses inside before a warm fire?"

"Sounds blissful. Help me up?"

He helped her to stand and she brushed snow from her pants. With a sudden wobble, she teetered and landed on the snow behind her.

"Cady!" He rushed to kneel beside her. "Are you okay?"

She took his proffered hand. "Yep. I have extra padding on my backside. Didn't feel a thing."

He chuckled and helped her to stand. "I do like that padding." This time he held her by the sleeve until she stood stable.

When Sabre thought she would start gathering her things, she instead said, "It's hard for me to think like you do. And you are…so different from me. It feels weird this…" She gestured between the two of them, then sighed.

"How am I different?"

"Financially, of course. You're a billionaire. I'm just… Cady."

His heart dropped at that sad statement. "You think that we are different because I have more money than you? Money means nothing to me, Cady. It's merely a means to navigate through life."

"Oh, come on. Your money opens up the world to you."

Yes, he knew having money opened him up to many more opportunities than the average person who lived on just enough to pay bills every month. But how to relate to that? He'd never known life differently.

"I shouldn't have said anything," Cady said. "I don't want to sound like I'm complaining. I'm happy with my life. And I'm pleased that you're so accepting and kind. I—"

Another kiss felt necessary. To silence her hopeless diatribe. Her mouth had cooled just enough that the first touch gave him a thrill of chill and sweetness.

Different from one another? Sure. He had more money than he knew what to do with. And she may have to struggle to pay bills. But that didn't make them different in heart and soul. And it hurt his heart to know that she believed otherwise. On the other hand, it set reluctance into her heart. And that served a warning not to expect too much from her. She was navigating new territory and he may push her too far if he weren't careful. As well, he didn't want to endanger his heart by wanting what he knew he could never truly have.

When he pulled from the kiss, her eyes fluttered open and she smiled. "You think kissing me every time I have a complaint will change my mind?"

He shrugged. "Maybe?"

She chuckled. "You may be on to something. I feel no desire to complain anymore. And I wasn't complaining, I was just pointing out reality. Ooh, I'm starting to feel the chill now. We should get moving. I need to work up some warmth in these bones."

Sabre helped her on with her backpack, and then she started ahead on the trail they'd made, calling back that she needed a head start, as he packed up the tripod and clicked into his skis. She was avoiding him. But it wasn't because of the kiss.

Or was it? Had he been too forward with her? She'd not pushed away from his kiss. No, she was reluctant. Set in her astute and careful manner. And that did not bode well for any future he may consider for them. Not that he was considering such a thing.

Was he?

CHAPTER SEVEN

WHAT A JOY to wake in an igloo! Yet, the sky was so bright. Cady almost cursed the fact the igloo's glass window had no shades, but then stopped herself. No complaining when she was on the trip of a lifetime! Something that might never happen for her again. So she'd accept the morning wake-up call with a smile and be happy for the day ahead of her.

A day comprised of what she wasn't sure. Sabre didn't go out on the job until night.

Oh, those kisses last night. A man didn't kiss a woman unless he meant it, right? Did that mean they were starting something here? But they'd only a few days scheduled for the shoot. Should they go beyond kisses, that wouldn't allow them more than a fling.

"Flings are fine," she said as she sorted through the sweaters and thermal pants she'd purchased with her credit card. She'd have to dip into her savings to pay off her credit card bill but it had been well worth the expense.

But flings were not really fine. Flings were short. Fleeting. Noncommittal. And while she'd never been one to engage in long relationships she also didn't do short. Seven months had been her longest and he had wanted to marry her and make her a stay-at-home mom. She'd dodged that domestic bullet but it had taken weeks to feel herself again and to not want to cry every time a country music singer wailed about sleeping single in a king-size bed. A month had been her shortest relationship. Even that one had left her feeling lost and alone. Chocolate cherry ice cream was good, but not heart-healing good.

Was it okay to simply have fun with a man and then walk away? Sure, it was. It was called being friends with benefits. Hooking up. It was making the most of it, as they'd agreed. But could her tender heart handle such a deal?

Already she was feeling something toward Sabre. Something possessive. Wanting. Kiss me until I forget my name. Get naked and take me! Whisk me away from a humdrum life and into adventure!

Just as she was pulling a soft red sweater over her head, her cell phone rang. Cady glanced to the phone on the bed, highlighted by a streak of cool Nordic sunlight beaming through the windows. "Mom."

To answer or not? It must be after midnight in

Las Vegas. She didn't want to do the time math. But she quickly did the day math and realized it was only another day or two before her mother had to go to court for divorce number four. Which meant, from lived historical evidence, her mother would be at her most needy.

Answering, Cady tried to sound light. She hadn't had time to tell her mom about this trip. Heck, she'd barely had time to make a call to her neighbor to keep an eye on her house; the eighty-year-old widow kept a spare key and had offered to water Cady's plants.

Should she pretend she was still in Vegas? No, she had never been a good liar. And there was really no reason to make up a story.

"Just checking in on my favorite daughter," Maria Burton said. Her slurred voice indicated she must be in the midst of a bottle of vodka. Her mom had highs and lows with drinking. Months, even years, could pass without her getting drunk. But when life punched her, she grabbed a bottle to soften the blows. "Did I wake you up? Didn't realize it was so late."

Cady wasn't buying that one. Calling in the middle of the night had never stopped her mother before.

"Uh, actually, Mom, it's…morning here."

"What? I'm looking out the window right now, Arcadia. It's dark as the inside of my wallet."

"Mom, I'm on a business trip. Our client liaison—remember Lynn Marshall from that pool party you went to with me?" More like crashed it by showing up with wine and an excuse that Cady had mentioned the invite so she assumed she was welcome. Not. "She was sick so I replaced her as a handler for one of our photographers."

"Good for you, sweetie. Working your way up in the company."

If only. A move up at Victory Marketing would see a pay raise and more interesting assignments, perhaps even more travel.

"So where are you? New York? Tell me it's New York. You're standing in Times Square right now. You have to eat at Junior's, Arcadia. They have the best cheesecake. Bring some home for me!"

"I'm a little farther away, Mom."

"Well, I've got a headache and don't want to think too much. Where are you?"

"I'm in Finland on a shoot to capture the aurora borealis."

"Wow!" Cady felt her heart flutter at that reaction. Her mother's enthusiasm was never forced. Such infinitesimal moments of connection were so rare to come by. "That's—wait. You actually boarded a plane? And flew across the ocean?"

"I did. And I rode in a helicopter for a desert shoot in Vegas."

"That's hard to believe. You wouldn't even let

me push you on the merry-go-round when you were little because you said it gave you a dizzy head. Wow, I'm proud of you, sweetie."

"Thanks, Mom. That means a lot." It did, and it didn't. Cady had long ago resigned herself to the fact that much as she enjoyed hearing kind words from her mother, they were fleeting and more manipulative than genuine. "I'm with Sabre d'Aramitz. He's a famous nature photographer."

"A man, eh? His name sounds French. I do love a French accent. Is he sexy?"

"Incredibly. And his accent is beyond sexy."

"Rich?"

"Yes—" Cady bit her tongue. But it was too late. She'd given her mom the wrong information.

"Yes!" Maria Burton's excitement probably echoed across the entire Las Vegas strip with that shout. "My daughter snagged herself a rich one!"

"Mom, it's not like that."

"Why not? Arcadia, do not disappointment me. You're on a trip with a rich man? You go for it. You take what you can get from him and don't look back."

Cady's stomach dropped. As did that fleeting feeling of knowing her mother may feel a tiny bit of pride in her. "Mom, I have to go. I'll talk to you when I get back."

"Only if you bring back an engagement ring. My girl's found a rich—"

Cady clicked off, not wanting to hear her mother's joyous declarations. It wasn't real. It was a greedy, selfish means to navigating the world. A trip that always ended in disappointment.

Catching a palm against her beating heart, she closed her eyes. She had begun something with a very rich man. Who could change her life. But if such a thing were to occur, would it be for good or bad? Was she even reading Sabre correctly in that he wanted something more than a few kisses between them?

An even worse thought rose. Was she turning into her mother?

Sabre texted his dad, Pierre, after seeing he'd missed a checking-in text from him. No response. He'd try later. Impersonal texts had been their routine for years. A means of showing their love for one another?

He wasn't sure, really, if his father did love him. Certainly, Pierre must love all his sons? But Sabre knew too well it wasn't an equally divided love. It didn't matter. Or, at least, that is what Sabre told himself, and had done so his entire life.

If only he could pick up the phone and call his *grand-père*. Tell him about the crisp Finnish weather and his search for the aurora borealis. And also tell him about the beautiful redhead who had entered his life and shown him a new perspective.

Yes, the perspective that he was missing something. For as much money as he had, and for as many doors as that money opened, Sabre realized it didn't grant him the utter joy of watching a woman's face as she experienced new delights. Like snow. Or fresh-caught salmon served on a bed of seaweed. Even the way her face brightened upon being told she was remarkable.

For as much of the world as he had seen, he oftentimes wondered if he'd become jaded. Oh, look, yet another cougar stalking an agile gazelle in the wilds of Africa. Or that stingray jumping on a wavy crest in the Great Barrier Reef looked like all the other stingrays. And so what about that exotic macaw building its nest in the crown of a palm tree? Seen it. Photographed it. On to the next assignment.

But taking pictures of Cady made him see with new eyes. He felt an unexpected return to his youth, those days when Grand-père would point to the ground and tell him to lay there and take in the entire world beneath his feet. The ants, the crickets, the microscopic invertebrates sidewinding in a small crack of earth.

There was a world inside Cady. A new place Sabre wanted to peer closely at and explore. A place carefully guarded, yet open for intrusion if cautiously approached. He needed that. Cady gave him a lift. Made his life less lonely.

So he started the day in the hot tub with her again. This time when the four-course meal was delivered, she dove into it heartily, uncaring about eating too much or dripping sauce on her wrist. They were foods and tastes she'd never experienced, and she opened herself to that. He watched her with admiration. She had relaxed around him. It was a mutual feeling.

After changing back into warm clothing in their respective igloos, they then learned how to ice skate on the resort's rink. Sabre had never skated and was not so talented as Cady. She mastered the balance and control quickly and even managed a spin. Was there nothing she wouldn't try?

Kemi also boasted a giant snow castle that was overrun by tourists, but Sabre insisted they visit. Not so much because it was a sight that interested him. No, he took his pleasure in watching Cady marvel over the castle fashioned from snow. Inside, furnishings and elaborate wall designs had been carved from snow and ice. Ice stools were set before a snow bar and icy blue drinks were served in glasses carved from ice. It was a little cheesy, but also too much fun.

Every time he caught Cady's glance, that smile,

those soft pink slightly parted lips and her bright green eyes clutched about Sabre's heart.

And he could not get enough of it.

Following Sabre cross-country tonight, Cady felt like an expert skier. Okay, not so much. Her quads ached and her arm muscles were getting quite the workout. But the world was so beautiful in its vast quiet as they glided in silence over the trail they had made last night.

Spectacular was the only way to describe the day. A two-story castle sculpted entirely from snow? Talk about living out a snow princess's fantasy! And she and Sabre had shared drinks at a bar made of ice and snow. All of it without feeling a bit chilled thanks to the insulating power of the snow. But really? It had been Sabre's presence that had kept her from feeling the cold. And his frequent kisses, quick pecks as he'd catch her skating into his arms, a sudden smack to her cheek as they'd wander inside a room carved from snow.

The man had a way of endearing himself to people. He easily started up a conversation with strangers. Be it a bartender pouring the fluorescent blue cocktails or an elderly couple sitting on the bar stools beside them, nursing hot cocoas. Sabre asked questions and was genuinely interested in the answers. And Cady felt her exterior armor growing thinner and thinner. That layer of caution and careful regard for anything and everything that might get inside and actually affect her. Letting some of it slip away felt freeing.

However, she wasn't about to skip naked across the snowscape. The resort did offer nude bathing at midnight. With free drinks, of course. She wouldn't even ask Sabre if he'd checked it out on his own. It was his right.

Now, as they landed at the spot where they had first kissed, she skied up alongside Sabre. Tonight, she'd brought along a heating cushion from the igloo to place on the rocks to keep her backside warm. There was something she wanted to ask him that she had been curious about since last night.

"You said you'd inherited your *grand-père*'s house?" she asked. "Is that in Paris?"

"It is."

"And you said you hadn't visited it since his death?"

He stepped out of his skis and went right to setting up the tripod and sorting through his equipment. "No."

A curt reply. Didn't want to talk about it? She had never been overly curious with strangers, but the man had become more than a stranger to her. They'd shared the entire day doing things that had made them laugh and hold hands and share many more kisses. They'd moved beyond business associates and straddled a line that she knew she must balance. And yet… While her body wobbled from one side to the other, it was her heart that reached out for a secure hold.

"Maybe you should go," she said while unpacking her supplies on the rock. "It could be a means to take in his memory. Maybe then you'd feel more confident with your photography. I mean, because you had mentioned something about feeling unsure."

He turned and flashed her a raised brow. Assessing her audacity. A glide of his hand along his stubbled jaw shocked her every nerve ending. The man didn't even have to try; he exuded sex. The key was to not melt in a puddle at his feet.

"You are being my therapist now?"

"No. I just…" Who was she to think she could solve anyone's problems? Well. It was her job to make people happy. And problem-solving was a key to happiness. At least, it was to hers.

"You're right. I don't know what is good for another person. I was just thinking about what you'd said about feeling like your work will suffer now that your *grand-père* has passed. If it were me in your shoes, I'd want to at least walk through that house. Say goodbye, in a way."

"I said my goodbye at his funeral. It is au revoir in French, you know."

"I thought au revoir meant until we meet again?"

"Exactly." He turned away from her and attached his camera to the tripod. The sky had already begun to green up and he knew that was a sure sign the aurora would show. "What more is there to say?"

"A lot. You can't let the house sit there unoccupied. Turn into a dusty old haunted mansion."

"I will arrange for a maid to stop in monthly."

He tugged the notebook from his pack, briskly. Obviously not pleased that she'd raised the topic. This was a new mood for him: defensive and reserved. Cady cautioned herself to be more attuned to his feelings.

"If you use your headlamp to see the page, please face away from me," he said. "Any ambient light will ruin my work."

She took the aluminum-bound notebook. "It's not so dark I can't see what I'm doing. I'll just tuck myself over here on my spot—oh."

The suddenness of the colors that flashed in the sky startled her. And then they took her breath away.

He turned back to her and winked. "Let the party begin."

What flashed in the sky was the most amazing visual display. Cady stood with the notebook clutched to her chest. A neon green ribbon of wavering light was edged with yellow and emerald. And above that color dashed a thicker undulating ribbon of crimson. And midnight blue. And a pale cream. When she heard Sabre begin his dictation of the details he wanted her to take down, she called, "Wait!"

He flashed her a perturbed look over his shoulder.

"Sorry. It's just so beautiful!" She sat on the cushion and opened the notebook on her lap. Tugging off one glove, she wielded the pen. "Okay, go. I'm ready."

With a nod, he began to call out his notations. The aperture clicked. He moved side to side, taking the tripod out fifty yards or more in all directions, and snapping many shots. She could hear him well for the night was still, the snow insulating the atmosphere. After a while, he ceased to talk. Focused on his work. A consummate professional.

Leaning back on her elbows, she basked in the glow and watched the colorful light ribbons dance to an unheard symphony. Maybe it was music generated by the very universe. She'd read that there were specific tones and mathematical foundations to all natural occurrences. Yet, the only way she could credibly describe it was with one word: *magical.*

After some time, he stepped away from his tripod and walked over to sit beside her. Cady hadn't realized how cold she had become. Her butt was reasonably warm, but the cold had seeped through her snow pants around her calves. When he leaned in and kissed her cheek, a fluid fire flowed through her. She forgot about any icy body parts and bowed her cheek against his cool bare hand, holding there until she felt his skin warm against hers.

"The sky is gorgeous," she said. But she didn't add, *And so are you.*

"Nature's dance," he finally said. "I got some great shots. The colors are incredible. I think your client will be pleased."

"I know they will be. Will you return tomorrow night? Take more shots?"

"No, I got what I need. And with the range of colors, the variety will allow the client to use many shots, yet they won't all look the same." Another kiss to her cheek; this time his icy nose sent a shiver down her back as she felt it at the corner of her eye. "There is just one scenario I'd like to also capture, if you will indulge me."

"What's that?"

"Would you walk out about a hundred meters, keep your back to me, and look up at the sky? Your silhouette will line up perfectly with the horizon. Maybe spread up your arms a time or two as well."

"I get to model in one of the shots?" She was

not a model by any definition of the word. Not skinny. Not beautiful. Not—

Cady, stop it! She'd told herself she had every intention of enjoying every moment of this experience, so…

"I'll do it! Help me up."

When she stood and her body was but inches from his, Sabre kissed her. Soundly. Exactly. No doubts that this was a flirtatious peck or spur-of-the-moment thing. This kiss meant business. And it did not stop. Nor did she want it to stop.

Cady melted against Sabre's body. His hand slid up her back, holding her firmly. Their winter wear crinkled with their movements. She wished she weren't wearing waterproof gloves that prevented her from feeling his heat. There was enough heat generated by their lips, though. A heat that curled through her cheeks and warmed her ears. It tickled down her neck and across her shoulders, a flash of lightning that did not disappear but instead burned itself into her being. Desire quaked within her. She tugged him closer by the front of his jacket. He moaned as he bent her slightly backward, taking from her, diving deep within her.

This couldn't end. Why did it have to end? He'd said tonight was all he needed. Which meant tomorrow would be back to Las Vegas for careful, concise Cady Burton. The fantasy would be over.

She still had tonight. Dare she go for it? Make it a night to never forget?

When he pulled away from the combustible kiss, he winked and gestured behind them. "Go. Wander toward that gorgeous view. Let me find your wonder."

Her wonder currently swirled in her core, begging her to seek satisfaction. But the man had switched from sensual to business mode in a flick of a lash. He waited for her with camera held ready.

Right. The business portion of the evening was not yet complete. Wandering out across the pristine snow that glittered like colored jewels, exhilaration filled Cady's lungs. Stretching out her arms, she tilted back her head and then twirled and shouted. A few more steps and she stopped and turned to wink at Sabre. He wouldn't be able to see it if she were in silhouette, which was fine by her.

Focus, Cady!

Taking in the sky, she spread out her arms. If only she could hug the sky into her chest and bring home the colors to forever possess. Now she understood why Sabre did what he did. Such an experience changed a person. And she knew she would never be the same following this wondrous adventure.

Cady made a leap, bending her knees. Tossed

off her cap. Fluffed her hair. More arms spread. She worked it as best as she could.

"Fantastic!" he called to her. "Perfection."

Rolling her eyes at his overly complimentary directions, she turned and wandered back to him.

"Can I see?"

"I will go through all the photos on the flight to Paris tomorrow."

Cady's heart thudded down her torso and landed in her gut. Right. He didn't need her by his side anymore. What she'd thought had become a bit of a thing between the two of them was suddenly replaced by reality.

"Right. Paris," she said.

"My home base. And…my *grand-père*'s mansion."

"Oh, yes, so you decided to visit?"

"Your suggestion makes me consider it. But." He pressed a hand over his heart. His breathes condensed in tiny clouds between them. "It may prove the hardest thing I've done. My heart already squeezes to think about pushing open that door and walking inside the empty mansion."

She took his hand in both of hers and held it against her chest. "Probably it will be difficult, and hurt, but overall, it will feel right."

He bowed his forehead to hers. "You promise?"

"I'm not sure I can promise such a thing, but I'll think of you, and send you best wishes."

"That's just the thing. I, uh…need you to come along with me to Paris, Cady."

"You—what?"

"I don't want to do it without you. In just a few days, I've come to feel so close to you, Cady. We know one another in ways others might never discern. Will you hold my hand as I walk into my *grand-père*'s home? You've brought such a lightness into my life. I feel I need that same courage alongside me as I walk the halls where once I felt such unconditional acceptance."

"Oh. Well."

He needed her? In Paris? Yes! But, no, she had a job. And if her work here was done, then she could hardly take a few personal days. Could she?

"You did tell me you always wanted to see Paris. And I promise it will be much better than a stay at a Las Vegas hotel with a fake Eiffel Tower out front. I can't lie to Victory and tell them I need you to assist me in Paris," Sabre said. "So it would be on your own time, so to speak. But I'll pay your way. You won't have any expenses."

"It's not the expenses I'm worried about." Yes, it was. She would barely be able to cover the clothing bill she'd tallied here in Finland. Her travel savings would cover—well, not Paris! "I'm not sure my boss will be too happy about me taking an extra day or two off."

"You were all alone in the office when I arrived. Still holiday, *oui*?"

"Yes, but next week everyone will be back."

"And yet, you were there when everyone else was away, which makes me believe you didn't get that holiday."

"Oh, I never take vacation days. Not even sick days. I just don't—" Have anything to do that warranted a vacation. Dreaming was about as close as she'd gotten to such adventures.

"Then you must have vacation days due. I'll talk to your boss. It will be good. *Oui*?"

Sabre was organizing her life for her, and that felt—not right. She liked to be in control and take care of the details. And having a client ask her boss to spend some personal days with him would not be cool.

"No, I'll call my boss," she finally said. Because… Paris! "I do have vacation days coming to me. And since I'm already here in Europe, it makes sense to utilize them and save on the flights."

"You are doing that taking-care-of-others thing on yourself. Does that mean you'll go to Paris with me?"

She nodded. Much against her better judgment—oh, who was she kidding? She wanted to go to Paris. But most of all, she wanted to go to Paris with Sabre.

"Yes," she said to him. "Yes!"

* * *

They skied right up to Cady's igloo and both clicked out of their skis. Sabre had set his gear before her door, and now he waited as she punched in the digital code to enter. When she started across the threshold, she didn't turn and invite him to follow. Had he read the situation wrong? But of course. They had just trekked a good kilometer cross-country, and he could hear her breaths huffing still.

His libido took a check. Picking up his gear, he began to offer her a good-night when she turned and asked, "You…want to come in for a little while?"

Then again…

With a nod, he dropped his gear and stepped inside the warmth of the glass-faced igloo. Cady stripped off her outerwear and tossed it to the floor. He stepped out of his boots and followed suit. When he stood in his street clothes and both had left a trail of gloves, boots and jackets behind them, he bowed to kiss her beneath the hexagonal curve of the glass igloo.

The chill left him quickly. Replaced by her apple softness and the utter deliciousness of gliding his hand over her supple curves. She melded against his body, further warming him. Defying him in a manner. Would he take her? Could he?

He wanted to. How to resist when they stood

alone in this exquisite location and had already shared intimate kisses with one another?

Suddenly, she broke the kiss, her gaze rising. Above them, the aurora borealis danced in maroon and lime. A swift ripple of light. And then an undulating fat ribbon of pale gold.

"I could stare at that all night," she said on a gasp. "But..."

When she met his gaze, Sabre's breath left him. Those green eyes were as if pieces of the aurora had been placed on her face. Dancing. Dazzling. When her hand glided down his chest, he caught it with his and then kissed her fingers.

"But?" he prompted. She wanted to make this night so much more, too. He could sense it.

"I..." A flutter of her lashes. Still, she maintained such direct eye contact he was quite sure she had dived inside his soul. It felt beyond intimate. Knowing. Warning? "I want to make love with you, Sabre."

"Yes," he whispered. And yet he sensed an unspoken *but* in her statement. Why was that? When she glanced upward again, he didn't want to believe the light show, as fabulous as it was, could win out over having sex with him, *but*...

"It feels," she said carefully, "too quick. Does it feel a little fast to you?"

"It..." No. And yet, if he were honest with

himself… Cady was like no other woman he'd had a relationship with. "A little?"

"I want you, Sabre." She huffed out a breath. "I can't believe I said that. I'm not usually so forward."

A blush rosed her cheeks. He nuzzled his cheek alongside hers, wanting to take in that sweet reaction, and whispered aside her ear, "Your honesty is refreshing." And it was. Even if it meant *not* getting naked. "Might I suggest we sit and watch the aurora for a while? Together? On the bed. But…sex is off the table. No pressure. Just, I really do want to snuggle with you right now. I don't want this night to end."

"That sounds blissful. Come on."

She took his hand and they plunged onto the bed. Snuggling into a soft blanket and nestling into the pile of pillows, they kissed a while and then stared up at the sky.

"This is perfect," she said. "And it feels right."

Much as he would prefer striping her naked and—well, no. Sabre corrected his thoughts. This was actually perfect. Holding Cady in his arms beneath the dazzling sky. A woman who could look into him and make him feel seen.

"*Oui*." He kissed her and nestled his head against her shoulder. "Perfect."

CHAPTER EIGHT

CADY'S BOSS HAPPILY gave her a week's vacation when she'd called, somewhat apprehensively last night, to feel him out about staying on in Europe for a few more days. She'd earned it, he said. And the entire office had a betting pool as to if she would ever use her mounting vacation days. So enjoy!

They'd actually bet on her at work? The indignity. But Cady marked it off as a Las Vegas thing. They bet on everything in the office, from sports to weather to who would get what for lunch. And now she had a week, a whole seven days, to spend in Paris.

Well. Her savings would not stretch quite that far. And she'd have to cover her own flight home. While Sabre had offered to cover her expenses, she could not allow that. They were not dating. She wasn't his girlfriend. There was no reason he should be expected to pay her way. However, she might concede to accepting help with a hotel for a few days—she had booked rooms for Victory employees; they were not cheap. But she could manage her food and other expenses. Likely they'd visit his grandfather's home within a day or two, and then, well… She may be on her own. She may not be. Not knowing what would happen next irritated her. So this would be a lesson in letting go.

Maybe not completely letting go. She still needed to keep a rein on her heart. Because allowing herself to really care about Sabre would lead nowhere. Really. She didn't even live on the same continent as he did!

Now, as she relaxed in a plush leather chair for the short flight to Paris from Oulu, with a snoozing billionaire beside her, Cady could not shake the trepidation. What was she doing? Was she crazy? Thinking she could actually afford a week in Paris? And expenses aside, she hadn't packed for this. She'd need more clothes. The rugged warm outerwear she'd obtained in Kemi wouldn't cut it in the most cosmopolitan city in the world. What was Paris weather in January even like?

Oh, mercy, she hadn't thought this through.

Letting her head fall back against the ultra-cushy headrest, she closed her eyes. Her fingers tightened into fists. Suddenly, this trip felt dangerous. Scary. She was out of her element. In a foreign country. With a man she had known only days. A man whose subtle aftershave tickled at her senses. It was soft, with an outdoorsy sweetness that lured her to tilt her head and inhale.

Everything about Sabre made her want to inhale him. Keep him for herself. Take more and more kisses. Imagine what it might be like to get more intimate, to hug her bare skin against his, to make love with him. When they'd returned to her igloo last night, she had wanted to have sex with him. But, as she'd told him, it hadn't felt right. Too fast. He hadn't seemed disappointed, which had confirmed her decision. They had watched the gorgeous sky for over an hour and—she'd fallen asleep in his arms. She'd woken this morning to find a note by her bed. He'd gotten an early phone call from a client so had slipped out to take the call.

"Just as well," she whispered. Would the morning have felt awkward waking next to a man that she *hadn't* made love to?

Could she have an affair with a sexy Frenchman? Her dreams had never dared to venture beyond her hometown and a simple life with a simple but stable job.

But the feeling of exhilaration she got every moment she spent with Sabre could not be discounted. The man excited her. He dared her to step beyond her careful boundaries. In proof, she was following him to Paris!

Knowing she wouldn't sleep during the flight,

she pulled out her phone to check the Paris weather conditions, and saw she'd gotten a text before boarding. From her mom.

Court date tomorrow. Wish me luck!

This would be her mother's third divorce. Fourth husband. While Cady had eventually decided it had been good for her mom to move on after her dad had died, after husband number two—right around Cady's eleventh birthday—she had changed her mind. Her mom was a serial dater. And marrier. She stalked rich men like it was her hobby. And a dissolved marriage didn't register with Maria Burton emotionally. One man gone? On to the next!

Clasping her phone on her lap, Cady glanced to Sabre, whose head rested on a pillow nudged against the shaded window. He was far richer than any man her mother had ever pursued. And kinder.

Cady had experienced the cruelty of her mother's boyfriends and husbands over the years. Those men had either ignored her or ordered her around as if she were a new assistant or errand-runner and not a stepchild. And when married, her mother tended to ignore her as well. Probably not intentionally, but rather because she was so wrapped up in the new man. And then between men, Cady was once again a planet in her mother's orbit.

It was, and had been, an emotional merry-go-round that Cady felt she would never jump clear of. She didn't ever want to make another person feel neglected because of her love life. Nor did she want to emulate her mother.

Accompanying Sabre to Paris wasn't like her mother focusing as if a laser on her next husband. Was it?

Cady shook her head. She wouldn't take advantage of Sabre. She would not become her mother. All expectations had to be shelved. Whatever she got from these next few days would be all she needed. And she intended to enjoy them thoroughly.

Which meant, Careful Cady must be left behind on this airplane and the new and aspirational Adventurous Cady would set foot on French soil.

A car waited to pick them up at the airport. They arrived at Sabre's penthouse in the Sixth Arrondissement and he invited Cady up to his home. A home not often occupied. A cleaning service visited monthly to keep the place polished, and stock the cupboards with nonperishables should he stop in unexpectedly. It was not so much a home as a landing pad between jobs.

He wouldn't trade anything for his nomadic

lifestyle. But to be honest with himself? It did feel good to step inside the marble penthouse walls and let his shoulders drop. Exhale. Set work aside. Here was home. Of a sort.

Cady walked ahead of him, down the long entrance foyer that was walled on both ends with a tall window. Upon deplaning, she'd shrugged off the heavy wool winter coat. Her bright red sweater was warm enough for the fifty-degree day. The window she walked toward looked directly at the Eiffel Tower, and had the—

"A bathtub!" She flashed a surprised gawk over her shoulder at him. Even tousled and admittedly drowsy following the flight, she radiated beauty. Her hair glinted in the daylight that beamed through the window.

Yes, that gray marble monstrosity could hold two people, he felt sure. Positioned before the window that took in the most amazing landmark in the world.

"Seriously?" Cady said as she stopped before the tub and looked it over.

"You don't like it?"

He walked up behind her and scanned through the window over the park below. Hundreds of tourists scattered the mucky grounds.

"It's amazing. But it's…right here. In your—well, I suppose this is the foyer. Do you actually take a bath here?"

"I've never used it."

"What?"

Her unabashed astonishment made him chuckle. "You can use it."

"You're darn right I'll use it. The view is—it's like you can almost reach out and touch the Eiffel Tower. This is crazy!"

"Don't worry. The window is treated so we can see out but no one can see in. You can stand there completely naked and no one will be the wiser."

Though, pretty please, stand there naked in front of him.

"But I don't understand why it's out here all alone."

"The architect's design. It's made of rare marble obtained from a private quarry in Greece. The bathroom is just through that door." He pointed to a mirrored door set into the white marble wall. "And next to that is my room. The kitchen and living area are through there. And the guest room is up by the entrance. You can stay in there."

Her head quickly swiveled to face him. "Oh, but… I had planned…. A hotel…?"

Sabre suspected a protest lingered at the tip of her tongue, but it didn't quite form. He hoped it was him that she was finding too difficult to resist, but when she glanced to the tub, he assumed his charm had been defeated by the luxurious promise of a good hot soak.

"I'm sure there's bubbles in the bathroom closet," he provided teasingly.

"I..." Still unable to make up her mind? The woman really was set in her ways of making others happy. Of not allowing herself a portion of the same. That would change, if it was the last thing he did.

"I need to run over to the family home now," he said. "My father is usually in until midafternoon. He texted me yesterday that there are some documents for my *grand-père*'s mansion I must collect. So that will give you a few hours alone. With the bathtub."

Her eyes brightened. So much more fascinating than the aurora borealis. Sabre leaned closer. Her hair brushed his nose. Apples filled his senses. He whispered, "And bubbles."

She suddenly gripped his shirt and when he thought she would kiss him...she said, "You win. I'm trying to enjoy this adventure and not be so..."

"Staunch?"

She winced. "Sounds better than controlling. And what better way to do that than to get naked before hundreds of tourists?"

"Arcadia Burton, you are a wild woman."

Now he did kiss her. And it was about time he had her out of that thick crinkly winter gear so he could glide a hand up her back and the soft sweater. He guided her body against his. Her generous breasts hugged his chest. The peaks of her nipples drew up a moan at the back of his throat. Could she feel his erection? He didn't want to be too forward, but it did feel as though they had grown close enough to get to know one another much more intimately.

Could Pierre wait? Of course, he could.

She suddenly broke their kiss, and said, "But I insist on staying at a hotel while I'm in Paris."

"Nonsense." He studied her gaze. Always trying to make sure others were not put out. A people pleaser is what they called people like Cady Burton. It was time she started pleasing herself. And he would toss her some pleasure as well, if she allowed it. "You're staying here." And just in case she was still reluctant… "I have a guest room. And I did invite you here. Please realize that it is no more an expense to me than buying a meal is for you. *Oui*?"

"Well…"

How she clung to her resistance!

"Cady, I want to show you my Paris. And…" Strip her naked and kiss every portion of her skin until she forgot her name. "But first my visit to the family home. Feel free to explore in my absence. There should be some edible food in the kitchen. When I return, we'll go for a walk and I'll take you to eat. *Oui*?"

She threw up her arms and announced, "*Oui*!"

Oh, she was letting go. And it was startling and fun to watch happen. Sabre winked at her and left her to get naked.

When he closed the front door behind him and started for the elevator, he thought, *I'm leaving a gorgeous woman alone in my home to get naked?*

That was wrong in so many ways.

But he pushed the button for the elevator, anyway. Seeing Pierre and collecting the papers for Grand-père's home would be tough. And he needed to get that out of the way before he could enjoy a woman on the verge of releasing her wild.

CHAPTER NINE

CADY HAD NEVER experienced such bliss.

Hot water rose to her shoulders in the soaking tub. Bubbles glistened iridescently. With her toes resting on one end of the tub, and her head on the other end, her body literally floated. A glance to the right took in the Iron Lady. Sabre's penthouse hugged the park surrounding the iconic landmark. She couldn't imagine how much the rent for this place was, but then he probably owned the entire building.

She was in Paris! The Eiffel Tower loomed just outside the window! Soon she'd be indulging in Nutella crepes and baguettes and macarons and… whatever other decadent treats the city offered. And the Moulin Rouge waited, Notre-Dame, the Tuileries, and the Arc de Triomphe. The Louvre! Never in a million years had she imagined she'd be able to make such a trip. It still felt so much like a dream.

Mmm… The bubbles were lavender scented.

Even more Frenchness that made her wiggle her shoulders in delight.

After Sabre had left, she had explored the penthouse. It was ultra-modern and sparsely furnished with massive stone tables and white leather chairs and a chestnut leather sofa. All the walls were marble, inlaid vertically with swathes of brushed steel. It didn't feel like a home, but rather a way station. And it probably was. Sabre traveled a lot. Surely, taking care of a real home wasn't even on his radar. Sabre was a man who could obviously live out of a suitcase, and more power to him.

While the idea of seeing the world did appeal to her, Cady did not think she could live as he did. With no home ties. No place to settle and put down roots. She needed stability. A touchstone. It was all that she knew.

So entertaining thoughts of starting something serious with the man was easy enough to dismiss.

But how about that fling? A few flirtatious days with the man of her dreams? In Paris!

Nodding, she shifted and propped an ankle on the tub edge. A wiggle of her toes spattered the air with water. The sky was bright. Winter-bare trees framed the iron tower. Ancient buildings majestically declared their history. The world was new and inviting, daring her to step up to the challenge.

"*Oui*," she said to her plans for a few days of fun. And not spending one moment thinking about her real life. "I'm in."

The family home was located on the Place des Vosges, one of the oldest city squares in Paris. Fashionable and expensive, it attracted only those who had the bank accounts to afford it. While no royal had ever occupied the aristocratic square, it had once been the gathering hot spot for nobility. The Hôtel d'Aramitz had been in the family for two centuries. It comprised over-the-top gilt and decorative ornamentation. Gold-threaded damask covered both walls and furnishings. Weirdly agile cherubs were carved into the ceilings, along with paintings depicting hunting scenes and even a copy of Michelangelo's *Creation of Adam* in the billiards room.

Sabre remembered sliding down the curved cherrywood banister as a kid and landing in the pile of pillows he'd arranged below. And exploring the grand hearth that could fit three grown men inside, standing. Covered in soot, he'd leave a trail to his bedroom where the nanny would chastise him, then scoot him off to a bath.

Not his mother. Born and raised in Iran, Pauline d'Aramitz remained something like a distant goddess in his memory. He could conjure the vision of a woman with long dark hair and thick lush eyelashes. And that was only because he'd stared at the framed photo of her and Pierre so many times it had imprinted in his brain cells. Had she ever held him gently and rocked him? Comforted him when his dive off the top of an SUV or shed had resulted in a hard landing? Read fantastical tales of adventure and derring-do to him at night? He couldn't recall.

It didn't matter. It should. But that had been thirty years ago. And life had quickly cemented his role from a very young age. He'd been the one in the middle. The son who wasn't smart or cute enough to win his father's approval. Sabre had been the son who'd had to break an arm, or two, to earn a few minutes of attention from his father. A pause from his work to note that one of his offspring was walking with crutches or had yet again taken the electric hedge trimmer to the valued cypress out front of their country château. The son who had dug a hole through the plaster great room wall, because *X* had marked the spot beneath the Louis XV wallpaper.

And even when Pierre had yelled at him, that middle son could only lift his chest and beam as he experienced the satisfaction of having won some attention.

Now Sabre rubbed his palm over the smooth curve of thc stair railing. He could still make the slide. But the faster he took care of business and left this house and its dismal memories the better.

"Sabre!"

He turned and greeted his older brother with a bear hug. Both stood the same height, yet Jacques was wider and thick with muscle from his frequent workouts. As an investor and accountant, the man spent most of his time sitting behind a desk so he countered that with exercise.

"Good to see you, Jacques. It's been months."

When on assignment in Berlin last fall, Sabre had invited Jacques to dine with him, knowing at the time his brother had been dating a woman in the area.

"What brings you to Paris? You usually avoid home like the plague."

Or a bad memory.

"Had a few weeks between assignments. Heading to Morocco soon. Thought I'd stop in and take care of the paperwork for…uh… Grand-père's home."

"Right. I wasn't sure if you'd ever claim that dusty old relic. You going to sell?"

He didn't want to, but really, what use had he for it? "It's something to consider. I have to think about it. Is Pierre around?"

"Up in the office. You want to grab some lunch?"

"I, uh…"

Jacques checked his watch. "I have to catch a

flight to Caen in three hours. How about I have the cook fix us something and we eat here?"

"I'd like that."

Cady would be left alone longer than he'd promised, but if he had to guess, she probably wouldn't mind the privacy. Yet, as his mind strayed to thinking about Cady's naked body, covered in bubbles…

"You all right, man?"

Jacques's playful slap on the shoulder knocked him back to reality. Unfortunately. "*Oui*. Just a bit of jet lag."

"You never get jet lag. What's up?"

He almost snapped out with, *What do you care?* But he held back. If he'd learned one thing about his brothers, and gaining attention, it was to never alienate them. Always he waited for his sneak-in, those few moments of precious attention.

"I have a, uh…new lady back at the penthouse. Don't want to keep her waiting too long."

Jacques whistled. "I don't know how you do it, Sabre. All the traveling *and* you manage to fit in a woman? You are talented."

"Yes, well, they never stick around for more than a day or two."

"I hear you. I have been thinking it would be nice to find the one."

"Really?"

Jacques nodded. "I want a family."

"You still with the blonde from Berlin?"

He shook his head. "But I do have a date for the family function next weekend. You'll be in town for that. Dad will be glad to hear it. I think he's already got a date set up for you."

"Another country-less princess or desperate heiress?" Sabre shook his head. "Good old Pierre."

"Right? I'm going to find Cook. Meet me in the kitchen after talking to Dad."

They bumped fists and Sabre headed up the stairs, hand gliding along the railing. Jacques was a good man. He deserved a family. Sabre, on the other hand, wasn't sure how to create a family. He wasn't even sure what a family was. The assortment of his dad, brothers, nannies, cooks and gardeners he'd been surrounded by all his life had never felt family-ish. It had simply been the situation in which he'd grown up. Couldn't even call it being "raised." More like growing into his own unique self *despite* family. So how could he ever become a father when he had no genuine role model?

Though the idea of spending his life with one woman did appeal. Someone to travel at his side, always there with him, sharing his experiences and the world. *Oui*, that is what he desired.

But did he deserve it? What woman would have the patience, or the abandon, to live such a life alongside him? To understand that he was always seeking and wasn't sure he'd ever touch that intangible something.

Might Cady fill that position? It wasn't a long stretch to imagine it. Though he'd known her a short time, there was just something about the dazzling redhead that beguiled him.

Sabre strolled into Pierre's office. The room was a seventeenth-century aficionado's wet dream with cornices, damask, elaborate furniture and even a stuffed leopard that had once been displayed at Louis XIV's Versailles. It smelled of cherry cigar smoke and bourbon. Sabre could get behind the occasional good cigar, but hard liquor dampened his senses. One missed a lot in life if they were not fully in the moment.

Pierre d'Aramitz stood before the far wall, his back to Sabre. A pinstriped suit designed clean lines along the tall man's lean physique. His attention focused on a bizarre painting that must stretch five meters square before him. It did not suit the historical decor. Blatant bright pinks, mauves and violets squished and squirmed and formed some semblance of a floral landscape interspersed with odd little globule creatures with bright green eyes. It looked too smooth and artificial, perhaps…computer-generated. Almost a children's animation on canvas.

Sabre stopped just behind the man and studied the monstrosity. *Mon Dieu*, what they were calling art these days.

"It's been months," Pierre said. He flashed a look over his shoulder at Sabre and an all too fleeting smile, but then back to the artwork. "Good to see you, *mon fils*."

"Always good to see you, Pierre."

Had he ever called the man Father or even Dad? He couldn't recall a time, not even when he'd been a child. The distance and lacking connection had always existed between them. Yet, the familial bond had made calling his father by his name the only choice. Something Pierre had never corrected.

Sabre stepped up beside the man. "Don't tell me Blaise convinced you to buy this…whatever you call this?"

"*Oui*, Blaise. He said it's the hottest trend. It's made by a digital art prompt engineer. You like?"

Sabre shook his head but didn't reply. It wouldn't matter what he thought of it.

"Blaise picked it up in Tokyo for a mere million," Pierre added.

Coaching himself not to choke on his own breath, Sabre winced. He didn't understand art. That was his younger brother's forte. Blaise had been branded with the Midas touch by the media and the art world, and whatever he suggested to his clients or called attention to seemed to become the thing of the moment. Good, controversial or, apparently, downright ugly. Digital art prompt engineer? Sabre didn't even want to know. He really didn't.

"It's good you're in Paris. For a while?" Pierre asked.

"A few weeks. I've a stopover until I head to Morocco for another shoot."

"Excellent. Then you'll attend the family celebration next weekend."

"Wouldn't miss it."

The d'Aramitz family held an annual party to celebrate—whatever sounded trendy at the moment. They put on a huge ball usually supporting one or a few charities, or to highlight a fashion event, or they'd even sponsored a motorcar race one year and all the attendees had arrived in outrageously expensive cars. Most attendees were investors in Pierre's business. His father owned a private security service that catered to royals, celebrities and even some countries' defense departments.

"Don't tell me this year's celebration is for this...art," he managed without sounding too unimpressed.

"The artist will be a guest, and his works are featured, but no, it's more of a celebration for all art and the work Blaise has done."

Of course, celebrate the chosen one. Sabre tightened his fingers into a fist, but when he realized he'd done so, he shook them out. He was better than this. Or he tried to be.

"You'll do me a favor and escort Ashayari Privat," Pierre said. "A socialite. Daughter of one of my clients in Dubai. She's in Paris studying fashion, and I mentioned to him I'd have one of my sons escort her to the event."

Inwardly, Sabre rolled his eyes. But this sort of request was nothing new. And it wasn't even as if his father were trying to fix him up with a rich, nubile woman. And then it was. Of course, did he ever refuse his father's requests? No. Because someday—*someday*—he just may earn approval from the man.

"If you insist." He'd done the escort thing before. It was just one night. "Next weekend?"

"Yes. I suppose you've stopped by to collect the paperwork for Papa's mansion?"

"I have."

Now his father turned and gave him his complete attention. The sudden connection, eye to eye, startled Sabre, and he took a step back, catching a palm against the edge of the massive desk. "You look good, Sabre. Something seems different about you."

Not sure what it could possibly be, his shoulders did lift when he considered the woman he'd left behind at his penthouse. Probably naked right now. Why was he wasting time here while a luscious redhead waited for him back home? Oh, right.

"Er, I came for the paperwork," he said.

His father went to his desk, a grand monstrosity that had been crafted in the seventeenth century specifically for one of his great, great relatives. Inlaid with ivory, the thing gave Sabre a shiver. He did not condone the hunting of wild animals for the esthetics of decoration and fashion, or whatever else it was humans liked to do with animal parts. He'd burn the thing if he had the option. But he'd tried once when he was thirteen and that damned ironwood was resilient.

Pierre tossed a leather folder onto the desk. "The title is there and all the necessary paperwork and deeds. Titles for the vehicles as well. That mansion is a dusty old relic. Jacques and I went in and claimed a few items of sentimental value. Hope you don't mind."

"Not at all. He was your father. You can clear out the entire mansion if it suits you."

Pierre shook his head. "I just took his watch collection. The old man had a thing for rare timepieces. Millions in value. I do like a nice wristwatch." He tapped the diamond-laden monstrosity on his wrist. "The place is all yours now. Fitting. You two seemed to have a close connection."

Did he detect a note of regret in Pierre's tone? Interesting. "We did."

Sabre picked up the folder but didn't go through it. His father had not acknowledged the intense bond he and his *grand-père* had before now. Because *he* wanted as much between him and Sabre? No. Foolish thoughts.

"Keys and digital security codes are all in there. But you already have those. You heading over there now?"

"Not today. I…have a guest waiting for me at home."

"A stopover fling? Always good to have them waiting in the wings. Just be sure she doesn't get in the way of the socialite."

Sabre hadn't thought about that. What he and Cady had was… Well, what was it? It had started as her accompanying him as a liaison for Victory Marketing. But their intimacy had grown. They'd kissed. They'd flirted. He wanted to take it further. Into the bedroom. But what were her intentions? Cady was not the sort of woman who did flings. And he couldn't imagine starting something with her and then simply walking away. It would be like walking away from sunshine.

But if he did begin something more intimate with her, then that meant he wanted it to continue. Was he ready for something like that? Could he fit it into his world-traveling schedule? Unlikely.

For as little as he knew Cady, he really liked her. He could see getting to know her much better and making their relationship more permanent. But that could only happen if she traveled with him. It would please him to show her the world. A world he knew she wanted to see but was too afraid to grasp.

She was not one to step away from a challenge. Might *he* be yet another challenge he dare issue her?

"Sabre?"

"Uh, yes," he muttered. With a nod, he gestured toward the door. "Gotta go. I'll see you next weekend at the party."

"I'll have my secretary send you Ashayari's contact information."

Closing the door behind him, he blew out a breath. Why had he agreed to that date?

Because he never refused anything Pierre asked of him. Because such requests happened so rarely. And because it made him feel good to have Pierre's attention. In a manner, his approval.

But if things went well with Cady, he foresaw a situation developing. Well, she was only on vacation for a week. She'd have to return to Las Vegas. Sabre could take the socialite to a party and then…

He pressed a hand to his beating heart. No,

that didn't feel right at all. Cady was too special to treat in such a manner.

"What is happening in my life?" he muttered as he strolled down the hallway to leave. "Am I..."

He didn't speak the words, but *falling in love* formed in his thoughts. And that made him smile.

CHAPTER TEN

As soon as Sabre returned to the penthouse, he apologized for being late. Lunch with his brother had kept him. To make up for the lost time, he whisked Cady off to a late afternoon of adventure in Paris. They snacked on luscious chocolate and banana-stuffed crepes beneath the Iron Lady. They strolled along a snow-slushed boulevard that hugged the Seine, stopping at most of the bouquinistes that sold books, old prints, sketches and tourist tchotchkes. He'd introduced her to his favorite craft beer at—surprisingly—a quaint little bar owned by Brits in the First Arrondissement.

They'd idled only fifteen minutes in a park because the benches were cold and even though the sun was high, the brisk air hurried them back to walking. Cady had prepared for the walk by wearing jeans, a sweater and the thermal jacket she'd bought in Finland. Yet, she didn't have time to feel the chill. Absorbing Sabre's enthusiasm kept her energy on high.

"This is a whirlwind tour of all the touristy stuff," he commented as they breezed through an old bookstore across from the Notre-Dame Cathedral. It smelled of well-loved tomes and ancient words. "Everyone needs to see it so they can affirm their idea of Paris, *oui*?"

"*Oui*." Not feeling the need to purchase a book, Cady shouldered up alongside him as they strolled toward a Greek restaurant that served savory chicken and fries all smothered with tzatziki sauce. "I need some of that."

He didn't refuse her a thing. They settled at a table in the back of the restaurant and made haste of a plate stacked high with crisp fries, shaved gyro chicken and lots of creamy tzatziki.

"I never would have thought I'd be eating Greek food and drinking British beer in Paris." She dabbed her lips with a napkin. "When do I experience the French cuisine?"

Sabre lifted a finger and winked. "We will dine in my favorite restaurant. It'll be a little scary for you, perhaps. But I promise you have not tasted better food."

"Scary? How can a restaurant be scary? Please tell me it's not one of those dining in the dark places. Or eating nude."

His laughter echoed across the restaurant. "I promise neither of those, but you will have to wait for the surprise. Now. What next? You want to wander down the Champs-élysées?"

"Is that the street with all the fancy shops on it?"

"Well." He wobbled his head, doing that Frenchman thing she'd come to realize was not a yes or a no but somewhere in between. "They also have several international chain stores, and I would not call those fancy."

She laughed. "Let's do it. You may have picked up that I like to shop. And I'm so thankful that you are willing to spend the time with me."

"Cady." His hand on the back of hers sparked like lightning crackling throughout her system. It reminded her that she was so close to surrendering completely to the man. Could she? Oh, yes!

"I am not trying to make you happy in the sense that you do for your job," he said. "I enjoy spending time with you."

She replied with a sigh and, "Same."

"Good. We are in accord. Then let's do the rest of the tourist attractions."

With the side streets crowded by tourists, Sabre took her hand and led her to a main street where they could comfortably walk side by side. His gloveless grasp was warm and firm. Hugging up against him, she tilted her head onto his shoulder. It didn't matter where they went. Being with him felt like the ultimate vacation.

Though he had made no mention of his grandfather's home. That should not be business, either, but she felt it was something for which her people-pleasing skills could really shine. Being there to give him confidence. Not that the man needed any.

Dare she think he might enjoy simply spending time with her?

Of course, he had said as much in the restaurant. Now, to really believe that a super-rich, sexy, world-renown photographer found it interesting to spend time with Simple Cady from Las Vegas.

"Have you photographed Paris?" she asked as their stroll slowed to a leisurely pace.

"Far too much. But there are endless wonders yet to discover. I will never stop taking pictures of my home."

"Sounds like you don't spend a lot of time here. You said the penthouse was just a stopover. Do you have an actual home?"

"Maybe? There is the family home on the Place des Vosges. My room is always kept tidy and waiting for me, but I never stay there. It's just Pierre who lives there when he's not traveling."

"Maybe your grandfather's place could become a home?"

He bowed his head but didn't say anything. Anything to do with his grandfather seemed to hit a tender chord in him. But he had specifically come to Paris to visit that mansion. A home, apparently, that Sabre now owned thanks to his inheritance. It would be foolish not to go there and, at the very least, sort things out and decide what he would do with the property. And she could see now that he might really need some support during that endeavor. Must be terrible to have lost someone who meant so much to him. Herself, she had been four years old when she'd lost her dad, so at the time, while she remembered crying and missing him, it had seemed to just become the norm. Now, she rarely thought about him. They simply hadn't had time to establish any sort of meaningful relationship such as Sabre and his grandfather had done.

"I have always thought home is where I make it," he said thoughtfully. "In a tent outside the pyramids in Egypt. Harnessed into a hammock supported by pitons on the side of a cliff. In the back of an off-road vehicle in the Amazon jungle. But there is something… Lately." He took a moment to close his eyes. His jaw pulsed. Afraid to confess to her? No, he was so open. And then he did say, "I do think having a landing spot is a good idea. A home that is not empty like the penthouse."

"You mean with someone waiting there for you? Family? A wife?"

"Could be. I'm open to everything. But my wife would arrive home alongside me."

"So your wife would be a fellow traveler. Wouldn't she get in your way?"

"Have you gotten in my way?" he asked.

Cady wasn't sure he realized the implications in that question. Was he implying she could be wife material? No. It had just been an example. He'd spent the past few days with her by his side. Though, certainly, she could consider spending every day alongside him, traveling, seeing the world. What a dream!

But only a dream. She had responsibilities back in Vegas. Like…her job. Keeping Victory Marketing on track was her superpower. What would they do without Cady the Receptionist Extraordinaire?

Ugh. Really? Her receptionist position could be filled by anyone. Not as well or efficiently, but still.

Focus, Cady! No thinking about work. Enjoy every moment, remember?

"I like being in your way." She walked out in front of him and turned to walk backward. "You're an excellent tour guide and—"

His kiss stopped her sentence like a lusty punctuation mark. Contact with his mouth curled a flame through her body. Paused riverside, her hip nudged the cool stone balustrade beside her. Sabre's hands wrapped around her back and pulled her closer. Close enough to feel his heartbeat. To smell his outdoorsy cedar scent. To be commanded by his overwhelming presence.

"I don't want to be a tour guide," he said. "I want to be something more to you, Cady."

She raised a brow.

"You like me?" he asked.

She nodded, struck silent by the connotations to that question and her racing heartbeat.

"I like you." He kissed her. Tasting his air, his breath, his being giddied her. "Very much," he continued. "I like you so much that I must stop calling you a friend or an assistant."

"You can call me Cady?"

He nuzzled his nose aside her cheek and whispered a kiss along the front of her ear. Shivers scurried down her neck, perking her nipples. "Cady," he murmured. And then in a deeper, more languorous tone, "Cady."

Uh-huh. Yep. She got that one. Right there. It landed in her core. And a little lower, where she felt her body heat and grow wet.

"I don't want you to stay in the guest room tonight, Cady."

The next kiss obliterated the previous one by luring her onto her toes. Reaching, pining, wanting to dive deep inside him and never emerge. His fingers glided through her hair, sending tingles from her scalp and down to her breasts where her hard nipples nudged his chest. She clung to his jacket, pulling him tight against her, but then smoothed her palms over his soft shirt, melding against the hard planes of his pecs. Every part of him was so steely and manly and…mmm, she felt his erection press against her thigh.

"Sounds good to me," she murmured against his mouth. And when a *but* teetered on the tip of her tongue, she dutifully reined it back.

But what happens when I have to leave and go home?

"You are very open to anything I suggest," he said with a teasing tone.

"You should know by now that I am a people pleaser."

"I do know that. What if I asked you to be lowered into a volcano alongside me?"

She laughed. "I'd follow you anywhere but into a volcano."

"Good to know your boundaries. So you will follow me home and into my bed?"

That was about as straightforward as a person could be. And she intended to be as honest and direct right back at him.

"I will."

He bowed his forehead to hers, then kissed the tip of her nose. "Let's pick up some wine on the way back to my place."

When in Paris. And with a billionaire who seemed set on treating her?

"*Oui*!"

Wine tote in hand, Cady walked, shoulder to shoulder with Sabre. They crossed the Pont d'léna that led to the Eiffel Tower. After taking in a few clothing shops that Cady had not been able to walk by, they had then both entered the wine shop full lust charge ahead. Yet somewhere while wandering the aisles, she had yawned. And then Sabre had caught her during the second yawn. He'd quickly selected a bottle and suggested they return to the penthouse. She was exhausted, and suspected it was finally some jet lag from the last few days of traveling across the ocean and visiting two countries.

But also, she was over the crowded tourist scene and desired some quiet. Not necessarily to be alone. But rather, to be alone with Sabre. Though she sensed the man could go for hours, all through the night. His energy levels were phenomenal. Being near his vibrant aura was probably what had carried her through most of the day.

They took the elevator to his penthouse, and he carried her bags into the living room and set them on the sleek leather sofa.

"I'll pour us a glass," he offered as he veered

toward the kitchen, which was open to the living room.

The area was two stories high and the wall facing the Eiffel Tower was all windows. Those weren't shielded against outsiders seeing in, he'd commented. Though Cady decided the angle from the ground-view wouldn't allow for more than being able to see their heads should they walk up close to look out the window.

Plopping onto the sofa, and pushing her shopping bags aside, she let her head fall back and closed her eyes as she breathed out. "I think Paris has done me in. I'm pretty tired. Sorry."

"No apologies necessary. You're a trooper. I expected the jet lag to hit you while in Finland." He handed her a goblet of red wine and sat next to her.

"How do you do it?" She sipped. What a delicious wine! It was smooth and warmed her throat with a lush bright fullness. Hmm, reminded her of Sabre. "Travel so much, and yet you seem to have boundless energy."

"I've always been able to go, go, go."

"That's another superpower of yours."

He put up his feet on the white marble coffee table and leaned back, turning his head to face her. Did his hair ever get mussed? It was thick and black and appeared to do whatever its master commanded of it with a flick of a finger or a rake of his hand. She wanted to muss it. Nuzzle her nose into the dark depths. But right now, she couldn't find the energy to do more than take another sip.

"I only sleep five or six hours a night," he said. "It's as if I'll miss something if I'm not constantly seeking the unsought and on the move."

"Maybe you have a bit of ADHD?"

He laughed. "Grand-père brought me to a specialist for testing. No ADHD. I'm just a wild and exuberant guy."

"I fed off your energy all day. It's as if when you hold my hand, you transfer some of that energy to me."

He clasped her hand and kissed the back of it. "How about now?"

Had she been so eager to hop into bed with him just an hour ago? Damn, this jet lag! "My ambient energy receptors are pooped. You're right. The jet lag has caught up. If you want to make something to eat for yourself, go ahead. I'm good for the night."

"I might order in a meal. A guy on the go has to feed his monster."

"Yet, you're so fit and..." She sighed. Sexy probably had nothing to do with the way he ate and took care of himself. Another sigh segued into a yawn.

"You really are tired. Well, it is after nine.

And you did give those tourist shops a good run-through."

She'd had to buy the proverbial Paris T-shirt, in many colors and with rhinestones. No way to prove she'd been here otherwise. Had she seriously forgotten to take photos of her afternoon adventure? No wonder her social media followers included only her mother and a few friends.

"You relax with your wine and I'll run down to the deli at the end of the block. They're good to prepare something for me if I pick it up. Sure you don't want anything?"

She shook her head, already feeling sleep climb over her shoulders.

He kissed her forehead. "I'll be right back."

Upon returning with the takeaway bag, Sabre tiptoed over to the sofa. Cady had fallen onto her side and slept. He looked around. No blanket nearby. This truly was not a home. Shouldn't a man have a cozy blanket to lay over his woman when she needed one?

His woman?

Well. Yes. Maybe? He was going with it. She was his…for now.

Setting the bag on the counter, he rushed to his bedroom and claimed the soft cashmere comforter from the bed, and then tucked it carefully over her so as not to wake her. Her carnelian hair spilled over one cheek. Her lips were slightly pursed. Beautiful. Luscious. One hand still clutched the empty wine goblet. He was about to extract that from her but didn't want to wake her, so he made sure it was supported by the blanket should she release it.

After he'd eaten, he then took a long hot shower. Slipping on a pair of jersey sleeping pants, he glanced in the direction of the living room. He'd had in mind to spend the night with Cady. In his bed. And she had seemed open to that suggestion.

Jet lag, the villain of tonight's story.

Shaking his head and smiling, he thought to call it a night, too, but he wasn't tired. He needed to go through the images taken in Kemi and proof them, making any necessary color adjustments, before sending them off to Victory Marketing. And also make sure the shots he'd taken of Cady were removed from the file. Those were only for his personal pleasure.

He heard a rustle on the sofa, so he wandered into the living room where his laptop sat on the table. The massive room was lit only by the dim ambient light from the Eiffel Tower, which allowed him to see her yawn.

She pushed up, noticing the blanket over her, and tugged it up to her shoulders. He picked up the goblet from the floor and set it on the table.

"Why'd you let me fall sleep?" she asked wearily.

"Because you are tired and it's night. Come on, Sleeping Beauty." He offered his hand. "Let me put you in a proper bed."

She stood and took his hand, pulling the blanket with her. "That sounds promising, you know."

"Oh, I know. Much as I'd love to tuck you into my bed? I'm not going to seduce a woman who's probably sleepwalking at this moment and just needs to snuggle onto a nice soft mattress."

She mumbled an agreeable sound and followed him down the hallway, past the bathtub and into the guest room. She sat on the bed and immediately fell to her side. "Oh…so soft."

"I treat my guests like royalty, *oui*?"

"*Oui…*" came out on a sleepy sigh.

"I'll just get your shoes." He slid off the ankle boots and tossed them aside, and when she rolled her back to him, he worked the blankets from under her to cover her up. "Good night, Cady, my beautiful wonder."

"Love…this…day…" she murmured. And that was all.

When she'd said *love*, Sabre's heart had stuttered. Love…him? No. Just the day. And well enough. Even if she would have said love *you*, it could have only been because she was caught between reverie and true sleep. In fact, she was out right now.

He sat at the foot of the bed. When was the

last time someone had said *I love you* to him? And meant it? Certainly not the women he had dated over the years. His longest relationship had lasted three weeks. And she had said *I love you.* But she'd also said *I hate you* when he'd told her they couldn't be together if she couldn't see traveling with him. He couldn't stay in one place and tend to her emotional needs. He didn't function that way. He was a rambling man. Always on the road and on the run.

Not on the run. There wasn't anything he was running from. Where had that thought come from?

His *grand-père* had always said I love you. And Sabre had known it had been true and pure. Had Pierre ever said as much to him? He couldn't recall.

A man should have some love in his life. It made him feel like life was worth it. Acknowledged. *Seen.* And he'd certainly like to hear it from a woman—and know she meant it.

He glanced to the sleeping beauty on the bed behind him. He could imagine keeping this going with Cady. They hadn't even had sex yet. And they'd known each other less than a week. Yet, that he could consider wanting her around without even having slept with her was something new to him. He enjoyed Cady's company, no matter the content. Maybe because of the content.

The conversation, the companionship, the camaraderie. And the kisses.

Their bodies were eager for one another, that was apparent. But had tonight's jet lag been an unconscious means to avoid something neither of them were prepared to continue? Because long distance relationships were a big no-no in his book.

Sabre strode out of the room and left the door open a crack. Out in the hallway, a pale light beamed across the marble floor. *Too much*, he thought of this penthouse. Yet, the decadent walls were filled with nothing that he cared about. Except...for her.

Might Cady fill in that missing piece called love that he so needed?

CHAPTER ELEVEN

CADY STROLLED BENEATH tall fern fronds that kissed her cheeks in a delightful flutter. Luscious scents of mint, lavender and rosemary perfumed the air. This private indoor conservatory was a *secret place* Sabre had wanted her to see. He'd photographed it when he was a teen, and had remained friends with the owner, now well in her nineties. The glass ceiling and walls kept in the humidity even while the chilly outdoor air brisked against the windows. It was truly a marvel.

While she had expected to accompany Sabre to his grandfather's mansion today, he hadn't mentioned it this morning when she'd woken to find him in the kitchen with croissants and coffee waiting for her.

She sensed he wasn't eager to breech the threshold to a place that must hold untold memories of him and his grandfather. And if that man had been the only one who had shown Sabre any kind of love as a child, and growing up, then Cady could relate in a manner to wanting to avoid dredging up the memories of such a loss.

Her mother loved her. And Cady had felt that love. But not all the time. Maria Burton's love had been cyclical. When her mother was not dating or married, she showered attention on her. But when in a relationship? There had been nights Cady had had to fend for herself, make her own meals and even sleep outside in the treehouse because her mom had whispered that maybe her daughter would like to do that.

Only when she'd gotten into her teen years, and had started learning about sex, had Cady looked back and realized those nights in the tree house had been because her mom had been having sex. At least she'd spared her daughter from whatever noises she might have heard. But seriously. Relegated to the treehouse!

Sabre would never treat her so dismissively. Oh, how she wished this fling could be real. To finally settle into the arms of a man who loved her. To know she was accepted and did not need to prove her worth to that person by making them happy. It felt possible with him. But something inside her warned her back from pursuing that possibility.

"You seem distracted." Sabre's voice brought her back to the lush, humid greenery.

They'd reached the end of a long aisle of plants and herbs and stood before an elaborate iron door. The tip of a pink petal teased at her thigh and she traced a finger along it. Had she really just walked through most of this garden and not taken in such splendor?

"Maybe a little distracted. It's beautiful here. But honestly?" No place for a discussion about relationship possibilities. "I was wondering when you were going to visit your grandfather's place."

"You are in a hurry to make it happen?"

"No. I like spending time with you. In fact, you can put that visit off as long as you like. Well, until my vacation expires. I sense it's a big step for you. And I will be there to hold your hand, just as you've held mine as I've taken some big steps lately."

He clasped her hand and kissed the back of it. It was a move he made often. She loved it. Made her feel like she was the only woman in his orbit.

"I know you will be a terrific support when I do venture across Grand-père's threshold. But…" He exhaled. "Not quite yet. Let's get something to eat, *oui*?"

He was all about keeping her fed, which she could not argue. And her hips had no say in the matter, so there.

"Nothing touristy today." He pushed open the

heavy wrought iron door and they walked out onto the narrow shoveled sidewalk.

The day was bright and cooler than the previous one so Cady zipped up her jacket and tied the red scarf around her neck.

"I have a surprise for you," Sabre said. "Do you trust me?"

Did she? Standing under the pale Parisian sun, holding his hand, felt...like the only place she should be right now. He'd coaxed her away from her settled and comfortable life. He'd allowed her to dip her toes into adventure. And he'd been a perfect gentleman last night when she'd fallen asleep on his sofa. Leading her to the guest room and tucking her in? Sweet.

But she was over their careful navigations around the idea of sleeping with one another. The jet lag had attacked. And passed. Tonight, she didn't want to be dismissed to the guest room. Tonight, she wanted to put her hands all over this man.

"I do trust you," she said. "But I'm a little nervous. You mentioned yesterday this restaurant might scare me?"

He kissed her quickly. "I promise I'll hold your hand. Come!"

Now that was mysterious, and worrisome. Hold her hand? To eat? What could the man possibly have planned?

Twenty minutes later, Sabre led her through a narrow alley hugged by two brick buildings. Restaurants and shops lined the main street, but this was one of many alleys that wouldn't allow for more than a single person to walk, sometimes sideways. At the end of the winding, snug alley rose a limestone wall and a rusted sheet metal door. He punched in a digital code and opened the door. Cady sucked in a shiver as they entered a dark hallway lit intermittently by red lights strung along the ceiling. She could just see his hand and grabbed it.

So far, the ambience was lacking, but she was in for whatever he had in mind.

"You have trust in me, Cady, remember? Follow me. The floor slopes rapidly. And it will become dirt instead of the stone."

The floor did, indeed, slope. And the air grew cooler. As her eyes adjusted to the dim light, she realized the walls were actually rock, or dirt. They were headed downward in a spiraling descent. The only places open to tourists in Paris, that she knew of, and that went underground were—

"Please tell me there are no skulls." Her voice quavered and she inwardly coached herself to be brave. If she saw a human skull, she might scream.

The man got his kicks by adventuring in all

the strange and out-of-the-way places across the world. And did she really know him? Trust him enough to follow him into a dark underground chamber?

Oh, Cady what are you doing? This is beyond stepping out of your comfort zone!

She tugged his hand and slowed her pace. Sabre paused, turning to study her face. The lights made his skin glow red, almost demonic.

Don't think about demons!

"No skulls." He smirked. "That I know of. Don't be scared, Cady. I've got you."

She swallowed. He did have her. But for what? This felt… What *did* it feel like? Like she was walking into a villain's lair? No. It was time to bolster her courage and allow him to lead.

No more Careful Cady, remember?

They walked for another few minutes, her boot heels finding the uneven earth a challenge, but finally she saw a golden glow ahead. Light! But where were they? And how far below ground?

Suddenly, their path opened into a small room lit by—seriously?—an immense crystal chandelier! One dining table and two chairs sat in the center of the room beneath the chandelier. The table was set with white linen, flickering candles and a vase of huge white roses. To the left, the light crept along the straight edges of what might be a door. A mirror hung on the far stone wall reflected the crystals and lights and glamorized everything.

"What is this?" she asked with amazement. She had stepped into a fantasy. And had been led by a man she trusted more every moment. Please, could she have this daydream?

He pulled out a chair and gestured she sit, which she did. "It is a friend of mine's place. He'll bring us food as soon as I text him that we've arrived."

"But there's one table. Doesn't seem like very good business practice to only serve one group at a time."

"Cady, this is the chef's table. The restaurant is topside. That's for the normies. We get special treatment." His wink worked like a flutter in her swelling heart. "You like it?"

"I…think it's weird but amazing," she said as he sent a text. "How far underground are we?"

He shrugged. "A story or two? The tunnels and caves beneath Paris twist and wend up to seven stories below. It's a Minotaur's maze. The catacombs that you see pictures of are for tourists. Cataphiles are the ones who squeeze themselves through tiny tunnels no larger than their heads and drop ten feet into wet and muck to explore down here. They hold underground raves, grand parties, some even live down here."

"I take it you're a cataphile?"

He poured champagne from the bottle, which had been chilling in a silver holder beside the table. "No, but I shot a photo series of these labyrinthian tunnels a few years ago. I like to think I am fearless, dropping into volcanoes and diving alongside whales, but I will tell you, some of those tunnels were so tight I thought I'd be stuck down here forever." He mocked a shiver. "We're safe here. Jean-Paul will bring our dinner in ten minutes."

"This is so exciting." She wiggled on the chair and took in the glimmering crystal array above her.

Sabre sat and lifted his glass. "To the most beautiful woman in the depths of Paris!"

Cady clinked her glass against his. "And to the sexiest man."

His eyebrow raised. They both sipped.

Let the seduction begin.

Sabre had never taken a woman to this underground eatery. He'd not thought to share the secret and wondrous place with anyone until now. And every moment he shared with Cady, watching her taste the new-to-her cuisine, sip the champagne that she had remarked would cover a month's mortgage and her laughter, it filled him with something that felt familiar, but he wasn't quite sure how to label it.

Something he'd once had, had lost and…

Ah. So that's what it was? Really?

Dare he be so bold as to think it could be?

"That was like nothing I've ever had in my life," Cady announced. "Who would have thought I would eat snails?"

"And eel," he added. The chef's specialty was smoked eel. "Delicious, *oui*?"

"*Oui*." Her giggles glittered, then she said, "You know I love saying *oui* to you. You make the adventure of that yes worth it every time."

"I'm glad, Cady. I never want my adventure with you to end."

That brought her ebullient mood to a sudden shoulder-dropping halt. "Well." She swept a strand of hair behind her ear, then straightened her silverware beside her plate. "That sounds impossible. You do know I'm only here on vacation."

Did she not want to see this thing they had started beyond that time? Had he mistakenly assumed the intimacy they'd shared meant less to her than it did to him? Hell, he wasn't the best at picking up on emotional cues. Yet, he'd thought himself to be closely dialed into Cady's cues.

On the other hand, when had he charged full steam ahead? Started thinking in terms of the unmentionable word…*love*?

"If this were to never end," she started, "that would make it a relationship."

"*Oui.*"

"So you would…call what we are doing here… a relationship?"

"I would." And yet his heart dropped to his gut at her actions. "But it seems you are not keen on that label so perhaps we should just play it day by day."

"No, I—" She curled her fingers over the back of his hand. "Most of me wants exactly that. A relationship. I feel so comfortable with you. I enjoy spending time with you. I—well, I really do think we need to explore that part you mentioned about having sex."

He shrugged but followed with a wink. His heart climbed a little higher. "Me as well."

"But there's another part of me that doesn't believe this is possible," she added. "I mean, I don't even live on the same continent as you. It's not like we can run over to one another's house every day or meet at the café down the street for a drink."

"I understand your fear."

"I don't want to call it a fear. Just, I'm always very careful."

"I get that about you. And I am the complete opposite of careful."

"Oh, I get that about you," she said eagerly. "That's what I love most about you."

"You do?"

She nodded, then bowed her head. If the lighting were brighter, he might guess she was blushing. And had she realized she'd said *love*? It set his heart to an interesting flutter, yet he cautioned that hope.

You've become Careful Sabre, eh?

Perhaps. But it was only because he understood how Cady's caution controlled her every thought and movement.

"I will take it slow with my careful beautiful wonder," he said, and leaned in to kiss the side of her mouth. So sweet there. All the dessert he needed. "Do you tango, Cady?"

"I…uh…don't think so?"

Sabre pushed back his chair and stood. He offered his hand to her. "Then I will teach you."

CHAPTER TWELVE

"WHEN DID YOU ever find the time to learn to tango?"

Cady followed Sabre's direction as they moved across the cobblestones set riverside and beneath a bridge. After their underground dinner, they'd trekked back to Paris topside and walked along the Seine before descending the steps to the cobbled sidewalk that hugged the river.

"I don't recall the year, but an elderly woman in Argentina taught me one night while I waited for a rainstorm to subside and head out on assignment. She was drunk and I was not. She left me with a kiss to my cheek and a few dance steps to my arsenal."

His hand pressed to her back, Cady stepped to the side slowly, in time to the music, feeling more than knowing what she was doing. They were actually dancing beside the Seine, outdoors, with dozens of other couples. Two musicians played a slow tango on violin and accordion. Three makeshift fires blazed at the river's edge, providing so much heat that they'd shed their jackets near a battered wooden trunk heaped with more coats.

But Cady didn't need a coat or flames to keep her warm. Standing in Sabre's sure embrace, following his guidance, she surrendered to everything. Wherever he might lead her, she intended to follow. And while they were not to hold eye contact for long, according to the dance, she found herself often catching his gaze, and he would pause to hold hers as well. That caused them to step off beat. Then they'd laugh and try to find their awkward rhythm again. They would never qualify for a dance competition, which was fine by her.

When a thick cool snowflake landed on her cheek, she tilted back her head. The sky glittered with soft slowly tumbling flakes. Everyone around them uttered a group, "Ahh," and continued to dance amidst the winter snowfall.

Snowflakes landed in her hair and on her shoulders. Sabre touched her hair, then leaned in to kiss her there. "Mmm," he said. "A snow kiss. That one tasted like Cady. I wish I had my camera," he said. "This moment is exquisite."

And only one thing could make it even more perfect.

"I think we should take this tango back to the privacy of your penthouse," she suddenly said.

Sabre guiding her in a circle, and with a hand

to her back, pressed her tightly against his chest. A masterful move that saw him looking down at her. "I think you are trying to lead, my beautiful wonder."

"Will you follow?" she teased.

"*Oui*."

Upon arriving at the penthouse, Sabre swept Cady down the hallway in a tango step toward his bedroom door. At the door, he spun her, and with a certain move they had both picked up while dancing beside the river, she leaned against his chest and he backward against the wall, angling them slightly in a defiant yet close hug.

"Takes two to tango," she said against his mouth. Then she kissed him as their bodies straightened. She slid her leg up along his, and his hand grasped her thigh, holding her there while they spoke silently with breathy kisses.

"I do love this dance," he murmured back.

Another deep lingering kiss stole any remaining caution that may have been stuck in her bones. This was not a night for caution.

Except.

"Do you have condoms?" she asked hastily.

"I do."

And with that, he led her into his bedroom lit dimly by intermittent flashes from the Eiffel Tower. The room was vast, the bed against one wall seemed like a distant island. The marble floor, flecked with silver specks, glinted fantastically with the ambient light.

He slid up behind her, gliding his hands along her hips and nuzzling his face into her hair. A satisfied noise growled from his throat, and his hand moved up to cup her breast. She eased her body against his and felt the urgency of his erection against her derriere. They were doing this. And her heart had never felt more sure of its direction than in this moment.

With a sway this way, and then that, they danced around the room, exchanging kisses, caresses and losing clothing in the process. When she stood in nothing but her bra and panties, she inhaled a gasp. Sabre stood before her, dressed also only in his snug boxers, studying her as if a sculpture on display.

“Don’t do that,” she whispered. She pressed the back of her hand to her lips. Though her heart raced and her skin was warm with anticipation, a flitter of nerves shivered within her core.

“Do what?” His voice had grown husky and slow with desire. Was it possible his eyes were even brighter in this dull light? And…hungry. “Look at your beautiful body?”

She wanted to blurt out that it wasn’t beautiful, but then…maybe it wasn’t *so* terrible? Cady worried at her lower lip. It was always weird getting naked with a man. While she wasn't a freak about being larger, anxiety did tend to strike in such intimate moments.

"Cady, my beautiful wonder."

He traced his finger from her thigh, along her panty, there, over the curve of her belly, and around to her hips where she could never chase away the excess pounds even if she ate salads for a month. The warmth of his palm, holding her, navigating her skin, stirred her to a shiver. And it felt—if she were honest with herself—so freaking good. Maybe he did see her in ways she could never truly see?

"I love your goddess curves." He bowed his head and kissed the top of each of her breasts. "You are a woman, and you look as a woman should. Do you not know that?"

"I..." She sighed as his tongue dashed along her bra lace. Her nipples were so hard. And—something flipped inside her. Now was no time to argue semantics, or what she felt about herself versus what he thought he saw in her. Her body zinged with excitement. Her heart had taken the plunge. She needed this man to take her. Right now. "I know that now," she answered.

He met her gaze and as he did so, his fingers slid down her bra straps. Holding her in his sight, the intensity of his wanting stare was the only thing that held her upright because it felt as if her body was turning liquid. Melting before him.

He reached around behind her and with but a flick, her bra dropped to the floor.

Fighting the frantic urge, she kissed him. Hard. His hands caressed her breast, drawing moans from her as she pushed him backward and he landed on the bed. Crawling over him, she kissed down his neck and chest and, oh, those iron-hard abs!

Forever or just a fling, this moment was hers. And she intended to make the most of it.

Careful Cady had left the building.

Sabre couldn't recall when after opening his eyes to a new day, he didn't jump out of bed and dive right into the hustle. Very well, so those weeks after Grand-père's funeral had seen him dragging.

This morning was different. Because when he rolled over his hand slid along Cady's waist. He nuzzled his face into her soft sweet hair. Fitting his body against her warmth was a ridiculous pleasure. He could remain here all day. He had no commitments and wasn't contracted to begin another job for more than a week. No one would care if he stayed in bed.

Closing his eyes, he nuzzled in deeper against her delicious warmth and softness and cupped his hand about one of her breasts. Heaven. He'd never felt so…settled with another woman. So completely relaxed and in his skin. She demanded nothing of him. Did not expect him to change his world to suit hers. She simply walked alongside him, taking it all in. And she was teaching him to do the same.

"I could stay here all day," she said softly.

He hadn't realized she was awake. "As you Americans say, same."

"Really?"

"You think I want to rush out and—"

"Grab life by the horns? Uh, yes?"

He chuckled, then nipped her earlobe. So well she knew him already. She rolled to her back. Her abundant breasts jiggled teasingly. Strands of red hair dashed across her forehead and cheeks. A goddess between his sheets.

"I'm not feeling that particular urge," he said. "But I am feeling another sort of urge."

"Oh, yeah?" She waggled her eyebrows, then turned and slid her palm down his chest and landed—oh, right there, where his body had decided to stand up and greet the day. "Then let's see if we can find a way to keep you entertained before the urge to leave strikes."

Cady strolled past the bathtub in the hallway with a wistful sigh. "I will fit in one more soak while I'm here," she promised the inanimate object.

What a life, to be able to afford the luxuries that would grant a person such comfort, to make them feel as if they were a queen.

Cady had always appreciated what she had worked hard to obtain. She'd never aspired to riches or to own fine things. She didn't even buy lottery tickets. Watching her mother's greed lead her toward pursuing rich men, and then seeing her crash land as those relationships failed—all because of material pursuits—had taught Cady not to pine for any such thing. It was the emotional level of need that she aspired to, something her mother could never understand. And she had lingered on just that level last night. Oh, so sweet making love to Sabre and feeling as though she were the only woman in existence.

Popping a few champagne-flavored gummy bears into her mouth, she then tucked the plastic bag away in her suitcase. Sabre had excitedly pointed them out yesterday when they'd been in the Champs-élysées' shops. He'd remembered she'd said they were her favorite.

How lucky could a girl get?

"Very lucky," she said with a smile as she strode out from the bathroom where she'd dressed.

Today she wore the soft purple top and darker velvet pants that Sabre had bought for her at a fancy shop. The saleswoman had insisted the rich colors enhanced her pale complexion and her hair. And the black suede ankle boots were so comfortable she figured she could walk all around Paris today. Living the life, and happy to have abandoned her careful ways.

Yet, the main reason she'd agreed to come to Paris was to go with Sabre to his grandfather's mansion. She didn't want this daydream to come to an end but…she wasn't stupid. It could never last forever.

Arriving in the kitchen, she was greeted with a bounty of pastries and juices displayed on the counter. Sabre liked to order in food. He'd probably been doing so his entire life. That made her sad.

"What would you do if someone cooked you a meal and had it waiting for you when you got home from work?" She sat before the counter and selected a *pain au chocolat*. The flakey pastry filled with melty dark chocolate beat a Blue Suede Banana donut any day.

"I'd feel as though I was undeserving." He toasted her pastry choice with a tap of his croissant to hers, then took a big bite of it.

"Undeserving? To have a home-cooked meal? You really were raised oddly."

"Maids, cooks, nannies." He shrugged. "It's what I know."

"But it seems you've embraced—" *the average people* came to her tongue, but she didn't want to put it that way "—the common lifestyle? When you travel you seem to take things in stride, not demand first-class or the top rooms?"

"I do not. A drive-up motel is as good as a luxury hotel room. All a man needs is a bed for a few hours to rest. But oftentimes the companies that hire me put me up like a king. Such as Victory Marketing. I am happy with either way."

"That was me who got you the elite igloo in Kemi."

"I know." He leaned forward and kissed her on the nose. Then he followed with a swipe of his finger. "Sorry, got some smooch on you."

He could get all the smooch he wanted on her. After last night's sex? Whew! What the man could do with his mouth and fingers was phenomenal.

"So what do you spend your money on? It's certainly not furniture or home-decorating stuff."

"You don't like my empty home?"

"It is sparse. But the bathtub does make up for lacking decor."

"You want a tub like that, don't you?"

"I'd be a fool to say no."

"Then I'll buy you one."

"No, you won't. I don't have room for it in my tiny house, and I already have a tub. That doesn't mean I can't appreciate a fancy soak when offered."

"Touché. Very well, no bathtub in your Christmas stocking. And you know that is the first time that tub has been used?"

"I do know that because there was some kind of seal thingy over the drain I had to peel off before filling it. Factory new. Oh, to be so rich as to own a bathtub just for looks."

"It did come with the penthouse. The former owner had purchased it, but sadly wasn't able to use it before she had a heart attack."

"Oh, dear."

"She had just celebrated her ninety-ninth birthday. A life well-lived, despite no dip in the fantasy tub."

Cady's heart dropped unexpectedly. "Did she die here?"

He tilted her a crooked grin. "Do you think the place is haunted? Are you afraid of ghosts, Cady?"

"I don't think so. I've never seen one, so I guess I won't know until that happens."

"Unless she was watching us last night, eh?" He winked.

She felt the need to toss a piece of her *pain au chocolat* at him. He caught it and popped it into his mouth. Dowsing it with a hearty swallow of bottled water, he then leaned his elbows on the counter.

"You want to know how I spend my money?

I have a charity foundation for the preservation of natural habitats across the world."

"That's awesome. But you're a billionaire. You can't possibly funnel all your money into that."

"I do not. Because, yes, billions are…so much! I cannot even fathom my worth. I invest, and make a lot more money, then stick it into more investments. Jacques, my older brother, handles my investment portfolio. Every time he reports to me, I've increased my wealth. My one standing order is that every year I give away half of my income. Most of the charities are environmental and focused on saving species destined for the extinction list. It's a small part I can play in trying to preserve the natural world that I enjoy capturing on film. It is not easy to give money away. It multiplies so quickly."

Cady suppressed the desire to roll her eyes, and instead took another big bite of pastry. If only her money grew so fast that she didn't have time to spend it all!

"Did your grandfather teach you to give to charity? Or is that a family thing?"

"Yes, Grand-père. My brothers both contribute to charities, but Pierre…eh…"

"Pierre is your dad? You call him by his first name?"

"I've never had a reason to call him Dad or Father." He shrugged. She could see his shoulders slouching inward at the mention of his father. Interesting. A touchy subject?

"We both grew up with only one parent. Parents that obviously were not focused on us," she said calmly. "You can talk to me about it. I understand."

"You do. I'm so sorry if your mother did not give you the attention you deserved as a child."

Cady finished the pastry and brushed her fingers together. She glanced toward the fridge but before she could stand, Sabre seemed to read her mind and retrieved a chilled glass bottle of mineral water and handed it to her.

"I wish I could have had someone like your grandfather in my life," she offered as a means to divert the subject. "He molded an amazing man in you."

"Thank you. And you will meet him, in a manner. Today we'll go to the mansion and—" he exhaled "—take it all in."

She clasped his hand. No need to say anything. She would support him as he had supported her on her adventure into the wild and daring.

"I've the property title and ownership paperwork. As well, all the vehicles in the underground garage are mine. I think Blaise claimed the red BMW, though. He has a thing for red vehicles. I might sell the others. Who needs more than one car?"

She shrugged. Who, indeed?

"Pierre and Jacques went through the mansion a few months back and claimed some items as keepsakes. I'll probably take my *grand-père*'s cameras and then…be done with it."

"You're going to sell it? I thought you were uncertain about what to do with it?"

"Selling seems like the only option. How else to rid myself of the heavy memories?"

"It could become a home," she suggested lightly. "Or not. You'll have to go in and see how it makes you feel. You want to go right away?"

He nodded. "Yes. Blaise texted me. He's going to stop by the mansion later. We should be on our way."

She didn't let go of his hand and when he stood, she tugged him to her. Pressing his forehead to hers, he smiled. "Making love with you, Cady, is delicious."

"Better than a chocolate pastry?"

"Infinitely."

"I agree. But I'm going to take one of these with me for the walk."

"I've made you walk enough. We'll drive today. You like sports cars?"

"I've never ridden in one. But with you, I'm game for anything."

CHAPTER THIRTEEN

CADY WAS APPROPRIATELY impressed by the Bugatti, which was painted with a color-changing sheen that shimmered from copper to violet as daylight played over it. Sabre didn't own a fleet of red yachts, cars and jets like his brother Blaise. And he didn't employ a driver, as did Jacques and Pierre. But he did like to take this baby out for a drive whenever he landed in Paris. Cruising down the Champs-élysées in his dream car? She handled like a dream.

Unfortunately, Grandpère's mansion was just across the river, so the ride was short. Parking below ground next to three other vehicles—yes, the red BMW was gone—Sabre got out and opened the door for Cady. As she stood, she slipped into his embrace, landing a kiss on his mouth.

"Mercy, that car is beyond."

"I'm glad you like it. It was a treat to myself after making my first billion."

"A worthy reward. I'm not even going to ask

how much it cost you, but I will forever lament any car that doesn't have a back massager and built-in champagne fridge."

"You should see when I flip the switch to transform it to a boat."

"What?"

He chuckled and pulled her toward the garage door. "Fooling you. Blaise is the one who owns that vehicle."

"Seriously? It's a car that changes to a boat? So you can drive on the water?"

"*Oui.*" He fumbled for his phone and looked up the digital codes he kept saved in the Notes app. "You want to take it for a ride? I can talk to my brother."

"Maybe." Her carefree laughter was the sweetest thing he'd heard in a long time. "Now I see the appeal my mother finds in rich men."

As he opened the door and stepped inside the dark entryway, Sabre winced. What she'd said sounded so blasé. And coming from his Cady? She had told him her mother was a groupie for rich men. Did that mean the daughter was as well? He'd not thought so, but he could see Cady falling for the allure of the luxuries that he took for granted. Would she turn into some of the previous women he had dated, wanting only what he could give to her and spend on her? At a moment when he'd thought to let down his defenses and welcome her into his life?

She stepped up beside him and said, "I didn't mean that. What I meant was... Oh, I don't know what I meant. I don't want to be my mother!"

"You're not." He stroked her cheek. So soft, and she wore so little makeup. All natural, yet her cheeks were always softly blushed.

"You don't know that about me," she protested. "I could be chasing you for your money. Just like—"

He kissed her. The best way to stop her from going off on one of her self-effacing diatribes. "It is true, I do not know all of you. But you know about yourself. You can be any woman you want to be, Cady. You don't have to be like your mother. You just have to follow your heart. But you can still marvel over the fine things. Enjoy them, even. It's okay to soak in the tub!"

"Thank you." She kissed him. "Somehow, just getting permission from you lightens my anxiety over it. You've changed the way I think about things. I've become..."

"A little less cautious." He kissed the tip of her nose. "I will have you considering that dip in a volcano in no time."

"Oh, heck no!" Her laughter burst out and he hugged her close because he loved how her whole body melded against his. "Now." She gestured toward the door that led inside. "Are you ready for this?"

"Truth? I feel as if I'd rather stalk through a dark jungle in search of a marauding rhinoceros."

"Yikes." She clasped his hand. "I got you."

And he believed that she did.

It had been over a year since he had walked inside his *grand-père*'s home. It had been his home, too. Never had he needed to call before stopping by. Always he could simply walk in, no knock. His *grand-père*, Gaston d'Aramitz, whose eyesight had been slowly deteriorating over the last five or six years, had spent most of his time in the small garden out back or listening to audiobooks. He'd owned three cats. Sabre wasn't sure what had become of them following the old man's death. He'd never cared for them, but did hope they had gone to a cat-loving home.

It pained him that he had not seen Grand-père for months before his death. Though he often sent him audio texts during his travels. The last one had been sent two weeks before the heart attack. Sabre had been standing near the Dettifoss falls in Northern Iceland and had thought the powerful rush of water that was used to generate hydropower sounded like something Grand-père must hear.

Now, as his footsteps slowly took the polished hardwood floor toward the main foyer, he found himself tugging free from Cady's grasp. He wasn't sure if he should turn and flee what made his heart feel so heavy or race forward and hide in the garden, as he'd done so often as a child. He'd thought it would help to have another soul enter this big empty mansion with him, but…

"You want to walk ahead alone?" Cady asked softly.

Yes. No. He didn't know what he wanted.

Yes, he did know. He wanted this tight ache in his chest to loosen. And for time to reverse. He knew he could not have prevented Grand-père from dying. Everyone died. But if only…

If only. He wished he could have been present when Gaston d'Aramitz had passed. He'd been told the home care worker who visited weekly had found him in his bed one morning. They suspected he had died earlier the previous evening.

"He shouldn't have been alone," Sabre whispered.

"What's that?"

Cady's voice coaxed him up from a descent into a dark place. A place of blame and regret. He had come here to face the ghosts and move forward. Time to do so.

"Grand-père died alone," he said quietly. "I was

told the home nurse found him the next morning in his bed."

"I'm so sorry. If he was in his bed…"

He nodded. "He must have known what was happening. Or, with hope, he took Death's hand in his sleep."

With a sigh, he gestured they walk forward. The kitchen was just ahead. Bright sunshine greeted them with a wink on one of the steel-faced appliances.

Sabre strolled around the long heavy oak dining table, running his fingers over it as Cady stepped closer to inspect the glass-front wine fridge. It smelled of tobacco and furniture oil in here. Not food. His *grand-père* had always been a light eater. The heart attack had been a surprise because the old man had not indulged and walked regularly. Rarely a day passed that Gaston did not make a trip up and down the river. His favorite park had been the Jardin du Luxembourg, up in the Fifth. But he had been eighty-nine. Truly, the old man had lived a long and fulfilling life.

Sabre walked past Cady, and as he did, took her hand and led her across the hall and toward a back room. "The study," he said. "That's where you'll learn who my *grand-père* really was."

Drawn by an eagerness of memory, he pushed open the double doors. He walked across the room and tugged the heavy damask draperies aside, filling the room with light and dust motes.

Cady took in the two-story room that was lined on two sides with bookshelves, a second-story walk-around that jutted out three feet and had a carved wood railing. A heavy desk was covered with books, maps and electronic reading devices that would allow the font to be increased. Grand-père had marveled over that feature. The easy chair still had an audio device on the arm and a woven blanket strewn on the seat. Bronze figurines of foxes, monkeys and even a kangaroo sat here and there. Grand-père would never hunt and unapologetically disliked anyone who did, including his own son, Pierre. The deep midnight blue ceiling boasted a marvel of stars, constellations and a hanging model of the Soviet Sputnik. Always a fan of space travel, his *grand-père.*

Taking everything in filled Sabre's heart in a manner he hadn't quite expected. It felt as if he'd returned to that which he had lost.

Kindness, attention, respect.

"What do you think?" he asked.

"Quite the storied old man, your grandfather. But what matters is, what do *you* think?"

"I think—" he ran his palm over the world globe fashioned from precious gems and minerals that he'd loved spinning and studying as a teenager "—that I've visited almost all the gems on this globe. Do you see this one here? It's malachite."

Cady peered at the globe where he pointed. "It's so tiny. What country is that?"

"Barbados. And believe it or not, I've not yet been there."

"You'll have to remedy that. What's that?"

He eyed the photo she pointed to on the massive hearth mantel, half concealed by a bronze fox. He plucked out the silver frame and brushed off faint dust. "It's the pika that befriended Grand-père and myself when we visited the Tian Shan mountain range. They are quite rare, less than a thousand left in the world. This was the day I learned that giving money away makes a man feel much better than when spending it."

"Your grandfather introduced you to charitable giving," she guessed. "To rescue the pikas?"

"We're trying." He placed the photo back on the hearth, smiled. A hefty inhale filled his lungs and he turned to give her another smile.

"You're glad you came here," she said to him.

"I am. Can I tell you about some of the times Grand-père and I spent together?"

She sat on the stool beside the chair, which thankfully she must have intuited was only for Grand-père to sit, and said, "Please, I would love to hear it all."

For the next hour, he regaled her of his *grand-père*'s adventures. How he'd been recruited during the Vietnam war to photograph the desolate conditions and had ventured off track and captured a rare image of a silver-backed chevrotain, a small deerlike animal. How he had met his wife while diving with sharks in Fiji—Grand-mère had been a marine biologist. And how he'd given Sabre a camera on his tenth birthday and taken him to the Tuileries to show him how to catch the light and mark his subject.

Cady listened, seemingly rapt, and Sabre found that speaking about his *grand-père* filled something inside him. He had lived those experiences, they had shaped him, they had been the true evidence to Sabre that he was loved. And sharing that with someone he now realized he trusted meant the world to him.

Cady could feel Sabre open up to her in a way he had not until this moment. Telling her about his grandfather lifted his shoulders, brightened his tone, and even made his eyes twinkle. His inner child had been lured back to the surface by touching the things he'd given his grandfather and relating stories to her about the adventures they had shared. It was obvious how much love had been shared between the two of them.

It pained her that he had not found such unconditional love from his father. Even his brothers, she sensed, were not that close to him. Probably things like saying *I love you* were rare in their family. She could relate to that.

But this visit was not about her. And it was easy to listen and provide quiet reassurance as he told her tales of the best of times when he was younger. And even as an adult, though Sabre worked and traveled often, he and his grandfather had been close. He had made a point to, at least once a year, take Gaston along on a trip with him, always grateful for his experienced eye and advice, even after all the knowledge Sabre had gained over his career.

After their chat, they strolled down the main hallway in the mansion. While dark with heavy wood and furniture, Cady could feel the magic that still lived within these ancient walls. Gaston d'Aramitz had possessed a whimsical eye. From the bronze statues of the most delightful small creatures to the artwork that featured ocean waves and macro photographs of snowflakes.

She stepped up to a photograph that hung on a wall opposite the bedroom doorways. It featured a monkey bathing in a steaming pool of azure water. Sunk up to its shoulders, its eyes were closed serenely, jewels of water beading its fur. It felt so Zen and as if the monkey were thinking, *Ahh...*

"I love this!" she said.

Sabre put an arm around her shoulder and nuzzled a kiss against her cheek. "I've never published that one. I thought it was silly but Grand-père loved it. It's a Japanese snow monkey. Snapped that shot on an assignment at a hot spring. Nagano was the city, I believe. They are quite the expressive little critters."

"I can see humanity in the monkey's expression. He seems almost more cognizant of his inner self than even some people can be."

"That is a lot to take away from a simple photograph. You want it?"

She twisted a surprised glance at him. "But it's your—oh." His grandfather was no longer here to enjoy the photograph. "Well, surely you'll want to keep it?"

"Like I said, I think it's silly. But it would mean the world to me to know it went to someone who receives joy from it."

"I do. I mean, it's just wonderful."

"Then I'll have it shipped to your place in Vegas. Make sure I get your address."

"I will."

A photograph by the world-famous photographer to hang in her own home? How exciting! But more so? It was a gift from her lover.

"Now come on." He took her hand. "Let's check out the attic where all the cameras are."

She lingered on the monkey as he tugged her away.

Yes, tiny monkey, I feel the same way soaking in a big tub of water.

And that was exactly where she intended to hang it: in her bathroom right above the tub.

Up in the attic, which wasn't tight and stuffy as expected, but rather boasted a high ceiling and was completely walled and lit, Sabre maneuvered her around many large wood crates and smaller stacked boxes to a corner that was neatly arranged with labeled cardboard boxes. Some cameras and tripods sat on boxes or the floor.

"Your grandfather had a lot of equipment."

"He did. He collected antique cameras. There's a camera obscura in one of these boxes. It's from the eighteenth century. But you know..." He picked up a more modern camera from a box and studied it. "This one takes remarkable images. You can't capture some things digitally like film does."

"Then you'll have to take that one," she said.

"I want all of these. Each one meant so much to Grand-père. But there are so many. I may have to hire a moving company to pack things up."

"So, you're definitely going to sell this place?" She'd thought he was going to think about it. And after his trip down memory lane, it seemed odd that he would make such a rash decision.

"I..." He set down the camera and looked around the attic. "I should sell it."

"You don't sound sure of that decision."

He gave her that wobbly head shake again. "Being here makes me..."

"Happy?"

He nodded. "This visit wasn't so devastating as I'd expected it to be. It's like my *grand-père* is here with me in this place. I can feel his presence. Hear his calm voice directing me to squat lower to get the perfect angle for a shot. Or to say yes before I think myself into a no." He took a moment to swallow, compose himself. Finally, he cast her a hopeful look. "Does that sound silly?"

"Not at all. Even more reason for me to wish I could have known him." She traced a forefinger along a tin spotlight that had been clipped to the edge of a wood crate. "You should consider keeping this place. Maybe even move in?"

He rubbed his jaw.

"It's not so close to the Eiffel Tower you can touch it, and I suspect there's not a huge bathtub to soak away your troubles as if a Japanese snow monkey, but it feels like you," she said. "Everything inside this home has a touch of wonder, marvel or whimsy."

He curled her into his embrace and kissed her nose. "You're perceptive, Cady. I like that about you. I also like when some of your hair gets caught up on your lashes." He nudged the rogue hairs with his nose and ended the move with a kiss to her temple. "There's so much about you to marvel over. I want to photograph you more. Promise you'll let me snap some shots later?"

"A girl would never turn down being photographed by such a famous photographer. But just for your personal files, yes?"

"Of course. Now, do you want to go through more of the house?"

"Actually, I'm feeling a little hungry. I left the pastry in the car. Maybe I can run out and get us lunch while you wander through some more memories?"

"Sounds like a plan. There's a place around the corner from here that sells sandwiches." He took out his wallet and handed her some euro notes. "Ham. And some wine, too."

"You Frenchmen do love your wine."

He tugged her to him. "Not so much as I… er—*enjoy* you."

He kissed her and Cady called that she wouldn't be long. But as she left the mansion, she couldn't help replay what he'd almost said. But hadn't said. He'd paused before almost saying *love*. Maybe?

"Don't be silly," she muttered as she stepped out into the cool air.

Yet, her heart replied, *I want nothing more than to be that silly.*

With a bottle of wine in one hand, and a bag of sandwiches and macarons dangling from her wrist, Cady answered her phone with her free hand.

"Mom." A rush of guilt consumed her as she stepped beneath a tree to stop and talk. "What's up?"

"The divorce is finalized. I'm on my own again."

"Oh, Mom, I'm sorry. You've done this before, though. You know how to deal with it."

"I do. But this time I didn't come out to the advantage. That rascal took everything. Literally everything. Including all the clothes he bought for me. I really loved those diamonds earrings. And you know I started with next to nothing following Number Three. I'm out, Arcadia. I'm not even allowed to go back into his house to collect the few things I can claim as my own. He's going to pack them up and ship them to your house."

Cady rolled her eyes. Just what she needed. Boxes of her mom's stuff sitting in her small one-bedroom house. "Of course, you can keep your stuff at my place for a while, Mom."

"Even me?"

"What do you mean?"

"Arcadia, are you listening to me? I told you I'm *out*. I don't have a home. Nowhere to go. I need a place to stay. Tonight!"

"Oh." This was a new spin on the same old disaster scenario she'd been accustomed to following her mother's divorces. "Well, I uh..."

"Arcadia, are you seriously going to hem and haw over your mother needing a roof over her head tonight? It is raining out. And it's late. I can hardly sleep in the park."

"It's just that I'm still not at home, Mom."

"Wait, seriously? You're still following the sexy billionaire around? Whoo!"

"I'm not following him around." Actually, she kind of, sort of was. Well, she'd done as he'd requested today by accompanying him to his grandfather's home. It had been—not exactly work. "He had something to take care of that required..." *a hand to hold* "...some assistance. I'm in Paris right now."

"Paris!" Her mother's whistle was so loud Cady had to jerk the phone away from her ear. "My daughter scored the motherlode!"

Possessed of a one-track mind, her mother.

"Mom, it's not like that." Darn! She shouldn't have said anything. Her momentary lapse into self-gratification had been a mistake. "It's nothing more than work. I'm here on Victory Marketing's dime." Not true. But to reveal that Sabre had offered to cover some expenses would really please her mother.

"Arcadia, sweetest, if you don't take advantage of this situation, you haven't been paying attention to how your mother works."

"Oh, believe me, I have been paying attention, Mom. Like it or not. I don't want to have a string of husbands falling to the wayside behind me. And I'm very thankful that all my hard work has earned me a place to live. Unlike you."

Cady bit her lip. Too much. She'd never spoken out at her mother like that. Had always felt it wasn't her place, rude even, to talk back to one's parent. Maria Burton was a narcissist and feeding her pride and agreeing with her at every turn was, and always had been, the only way to keep the calm between them. At the sacrifice of Cady's own well-being.

Had a few days away from Las Vegas changed something inside her? Straightened her spine? Made her more willing to stand up to her mother?

Apparently so. And…she didn't feel like an apology was due.

After an awkward silence, her mother finally said, "So you're not going to let me stay with you?"

With a sigh, Cady dropped her shoulders. She

was not cruel. But if she had a tree house in her backyard, she would certainly consider suggesting her mom stay in that for the night.

"You can stay, Mom. I'll text Mrs. Henderson next door and tell her to give you my key. You can sleep on the pullout sofa in the living room."

"Not your bed? I mean, if you're not home..."

"Whatever, Mom. Do what works for you. Just...please don't crank up the heat like you always do. I need to keep the energy bill to a minimum."

"Bills get paid when your man is making billions. I'm just saying, sweetie."

Yes, they did get paid. But a woman also risked losing her house and everything she owned when that relationship went sour. Depending on a rich man for everything? Never going to happen.

"I have to go. The client is waiting for me."

"You call him the client? Arcadia, now listen."

"What?"

Her mother's heavy exhale preceded, "I know you've had an interesting life living with me."

Interesting was putting it mildly.

"I like rich men," her mother said plainly. "What can I say? The way I live my life? It works for me. It is what I know. What I've always known. But I do know I wasn't always there for you."

So many times.

"You're an adult now. You don't need a mother."

Cady wouldn't go that far. Everyone needed a mother. A safe landing. A comforting hug. Maybe someday her mom would transform into something like that? Cady wouldn't hold her breath. She'd never beaten her, and hadn't kicked her out to survive on the streets. So many kids had it much worse when growing up.

"You deserve a wonderful life," her mother said. "And you can have that with this photographer. You just have to be receptive to what he says, pick up on his emotions, his needs—"

"Mom, the last thing I want from you is dating advice."

"So you two are dating? Yes! Now, how can we ensure you won't let this big fish slip from the hook?"

"There's no hook! It's just…a fling."

"Don't say that, Arcadia. You can do this—"

"I'm going to hang up now, Mom. Go ahead and sleep in my bed. I'll see you in a few days when my work in Paris is done. Goodbye."

Tucking away her phone, Cady swore quietly and shook her head. She'd narrowly avoided hearing Maria Burton's Top Ten Ways to Hook a Man.

"Is that what I'm doing?"

She had attracted a rich man's attention. And she'd begun to think in terms of how fabulous it might be should it become a relationship. Big bathtubs. Fancy wine. Food delivered whenever you wanted it. Fast expensive cars. Traveling the world. Dancing tango under the falling snow!

And all she had to do was hook him.

"I won't do that to him. He's a kind, loving man. The way he sees the world…" She really liked Sabre. More than like. "But…"

But even if they could figure out how to have a long-distance relationship, she'd always hear her mother's voice yelling triumphantly that her daughter had scored a rich man. And Cady did not want to end up kicked to the curb, seeking help from others because the man she had grown to depend on had cut her off.

She had created a life for herself in Las Vegas. A small life. A simple life.

Not the adventurous life you dream about.

Was it too late to rewind and refuse to go along with Sabre to Finland? Yes.

Was it too late to stop whatever had started between them in its tracks before it hurt her? Maybe. Maybe not.

The red flag her mother's phone call had raised flapped madly in her thoughts.

But how to walk away when she knew she had already fallen for Sabre?

CHAPTER FOURTEEN

CADY ENTERED THE mansion through the front door and saw Sabre in the foyer fist-bumping another man. Must be the brother he said was stopping by. She waved and pointed to the bag of sandwiches and then to the kitchen to indicate she would leave them to themselves. On her way, she noticed a missed text on her phone. From her boss at Victory. Hmm…

"Cady, come meet my brother Blaise," Sabre called. "Come!"

Slashing the message app closed before she could read the text, she swung around and headed back into the foyer. Meeting the family already? While half of her was excited to see more into Sabre's life and his family, the other half still waved that red flag. *Danger, Cady Burton. Be careful. You must not become your mother!*

"Blaise, this is the woman I told you about. Cady, my youngest brother, Blaise."

A man of equal handsomeness to Sabre, same

height, same gorgeously tanned skin and jet hair, smiled warmly and leaned in to buss both her cheeks. Another delicious-smelling man. Must be something in the family genes.

"Pleasure to meet you, Cady. Sabre tells me you are enjoying an adventure."

"I am. I've never been overseas. Finland and France in less than a week is a lot to take in."

"But you will love Paris?"

"I will and I do. Are you the brother who is the art dealer?"

"Blaise has the Midas touch," Sabre offered. "Whatever he touches sells for millions. He's got a savant brain for all things artistic."

Blaise shrugged shyly. Cady liked him for his modesty. And how on earth did both brothers, so handsomely sexy, manage to be currently single?

Well, Sabre wasn't exactly single. He was… Could she call him hers? No, she had to stop thinking like that. *Just a fling, Cady!*

"Did you bring sandwiches?" Sabre asked as he eyed her bag.

"Yes, and I bought a couple extra and some macarons so Blaise can join us for lunch."

"I will," Blaise said. "I take it you two are not a couple?" he then asked.

Sabre said, "Right now we are." He glanced to Cady and winked.

Right now? As in only when she was here in

Paris? Is that what that wink meant? Oh, dear. Despite her better senses and the need to not be her mother, she really did want them to be a couple. She'd never felt so free and comfortable than when she was with Sabre. He had opened her up like a book long in need of having its spine cracked and its pages aired out.

"But are you not accompanying Ashayari Privat to the family event next weekend?" Blaise asked his brother. "She is a recent move to Paris to study modeling," he said to Cady.

"A model, eh?" Cady tried teasingly.

But her heart took a dive at hearing that Sabre had a date. She couldn't show a reaction. She would not allow him to see how it hurt her to know he had a date on the books for the near future. How wrong she had been to think he could even consider them a couple!

Sabre waved it off with a sweep of his hand. "We have a family party once a year. Pierre asked me to take some socialite, as he has done many times previously. I do what he asks and keep the waves calm between us. It means nothing. Now let me show you the pieces in Grand-père's study that I think I will sell," he said to his brother. Then to Cady he said, "Would you bring the sandwiches to the kitchen and then catch up with us?"

"Of course."

The men wandered off, and Cady unclenched her grip on the bag. How she had not managed to drop the wine bottle was beyond her. It was only after the brothers had turned a corner that she swallowed and made a little gasping noise. Fear and hurt had gotten stuck at the back of her throat. Thankfully, those emotions hadn't come out as a scream. Keeping her emotions close and restrained was ladylike and the only way to please others.

And if she couldn't keep everyone around her happy, then she couldn't be happy.

No. That wasn't true. Cady had begun to realize that it was okay to make herself happy before others. Yet, just now she'd been punished for such daring. Sabre dismissed her as an aside. That was how it felt. As if he'd jammed a camera tripod right through her heart.

Wandering into the kitchen, she set the bag on the counter, then leaned forward, catching her elbows on the cool marble. A tear puddled at the corner of one eye. Biting her lip, she quickly swiped it away. A glance over her shoulder confirmed she was still alone.

She muttered the worst swear word she could summon. Her mother would be so proud.

Sabre had a date with a model? For a big family party? She couldn't compete with a model. Did she *want* to compete for the man?

She could barely think the answer, but her head was nodding. Yes, oh, yes, she wanted that man. But he could never be hers. She didn't travel in the same social stratosphere as he did. He may be adventurous, a vagabond world traveler. But that didn't mean he didn't desire stability and someone of his equal social status to keep him happy. Like a gorgeous model.

Something she could never be. Had Sabre's sweet words about loving her curvy body simply been a means to get something from her? Between the sheets? A means to satisfaction? Ugh!

And yet, she had been an accomplice to that passion-spurred night. She had wanted him equally. The blame rested firmly on both of them. They'd conspired to make the most of it, and they had.

And now it was over.

She tugged out her phone and clicked to the airline website she always used. It was foolish to remain in Paris now that she'd done as Sabre had asked. He'd survived the trip down memory lane. And he was moving forward. With a model.

Certainly, she couldn't use Victory Marketing's account to fly home. If she wanted to hop a plane, she'd have to borrow some cash from her savings. But did she even have enough? All the clothing she had purchased had come out of her account.

Quickly, she switched to her bank app and checked her balance. "That's not right." It didn't show an entry for her purchases at the Kemi clothing store. How was that possible? Surely, it would have posted by now.

"Cady."

Spinning at the sound of Sabre's voice, she tucked away her phone in a pocket. She didn't see the brother behind him as he entered the kitchen.

He walked up to her, put his arms around her and kissed her. Too quickly. "You like my brother?"

"He seems nice. Very handsome, like you. Did you… My clothing purchases in Kemi don't show in my bank account. Did you…switch our cards?"

"Yes." He eyed the bag. "Did you get ham?"

"Of course. But why would you do that? Pay for me?"

"Because I wanted to." He pulled a wrapped sandwich out from the bag and the aroma of mustard crept out. "And macarons? Cady, you are the best."

"You know I aim to please."

She couldn't even beat up herself for saying such a thing. Because it was true. Cady Burton only knew how to please others. And that was obviously her lot in life. Accept it. Live with it.

He'd paid for her clothes? And she knew arguing about it now would get her nowhere. The expense obviously meant little to him, and it had been a kind gesture. But he should have asked.

Is this what her mother expected from her men? To buy her things? To send her out for sandwiches and repay her menial tasks with gifts?

It felt wrong. Not at all what Cady wanted in a caring, genuine relationship.

"So, uh…" She rubbed the back of her neck, waffling. Oh, hell. Out with it! "I was thinking about getting a flight back to Vegas as soon as possible."

Sabre dropped the sandwich. His gape spoke volumes.

"Well, I don't know what more you need me for. And it seems like you have a date next weekend. Which means that we—Oh, it doesn't matter. I'm no longer needed here. And I don't want to get in your way."

"Cady." He took her hands and studied her face. Those whiskey brown eyes held such depth and flecks of gold. "Are you angry that I paid for your clothing?"

"No. Yes. I mean…it's not about that, it's…"

"Does learning about my date with Ashayari make you jealous?"

"Well…" Yes! Was he that blind? "I…"

"It does. *Bien.*"

Bien? What did *bien* mean? Oh! Cady narrowed her gaze at him. "Why *good*?"

"Because that means you like me."

"I do like you."

"Then why do you want to leave me?"

"Because, Sabre, you're…"

Everything she could ever desire in a man. And more. He had the perfect life. He had a life she wanted. And he knew how to make love to her better than any man ever had. Sabre d'Aramitz *knew* her body. And they tangoed not too terribly together. And he was always encouraging her to take a leap.

And yet. "What exactly do we have going on between us? Because it can't be something serious. Something that we expect to develop and grow."

"Why not?"

She gaped at him. "You literally just said you're taking a model on a date. Do the French do things differently? Is juggling two women a common thing for you? Because I like exclusive rights when I'm dating a man."

"We are dating, *oui*?" A hint of whimsy lifted his eyebrow, as she'd learned was a tell for his more playful moods.

"Sabre." He was so frustrating! He wasn't getting why she felt so awful.

Then maybe you'd better tell him. Remember, Careful Cady has left the building.

She waved her hand dismissively. "I'm just a little off balance right now. Because of you."

"My apologies—"

"No. Let me speak. Because if I don't say this now, I never will. Sabre, I like you. A lot. And if truth be told, I would like this—" she gestured frantically back and forth between them "—to be...something."

"Agreed."

"Really?"

She didn't know what to say. It all felt too big and immense, and yet so small and precious at the same time. And it was all topped off by that big red flag with her mother's name on it. If Sabre had another woman, he would ignore Cady for something better. Just as her mom accepted such treatment from her dates, lovers, and husbands. Just as Cady had learned to accept through the years. "I'm just...unsure. There's so much..." Holding her back?

"The model thing is just a favor to my father," he reassured. "Pierre asked me to accompany her when I went to the house yesterday. It's not a date like a boyfriend-girlfriend scenario."

"Well. Okay. But."

That teasing brow of his rose again. Oh, how she wanted to kiss him right now. Change his mind about having any other woman but her. She could do it. But unlike his manner of silencing her with a kiss whenever she was ready to step back from the leap, she didn't want to do the same.

"If we were a thing," she said, "A couple."

"We can be."

"Then I certainly wouldn't want you to take another woman to a party. No matter if your father did ask you to do it as a favor."

"I see." He stepped back and shoved his hands in his front trouser pockets.

"I don't want to make a fuss about it," she said. "I have no right to ask for what I want from you. And you should probably get back to your brother."

"Cady, you must always ask for what you desire. And we need to get this right," he insisted.

"I agree. But your brother…" At that moment, the clatter of footsteps echoed closer in the hallway. Cady picked up the sandwich bag. "Let's save these for later, at your penthouse. Then we can talk about this?"

"Very well. But." He raised one finger. "Just one kiss?"

She pouted for a moment. Nothing had been resolved. He still had a date with a model. And she was still unsure where, exactly, they stood with one another. But. "Anything for you."

* * *

During the drive back to his penthouse, Sabre received a text from Pierre. It provided Ashayari's number and address.

Please call her a day or two before the party. She will appreciate your attention.

Swearing to himself, he tucked away the phone. Blaise should not have mentioned the date in front of Cady. It had upset her. And…he wasn't sure if he would have told her about it had he been given a choice. It was, truly, in his mind, just a favor. But he could understand how Cady, any woman, would see it differently.

"Everything okay?" she asked. Her attention was on her cell phone, typing in a text or something.

"*Oui.*"

Not really.

What was he doing? Juggling two women at once? It wasn't as though he were involved with Ashayari. On the other hand, Pierre never did anything without reason. On many occasions, Pierre had attempted his hand at matchmaking for his sons. Jacques had actually dated one of their father's selections for over a year. That had ended disastrously. Women who sought men merely for their money, no matter how sincere they appeared on the surface, always eventually revealed themselves. In the most horrific of ways. Jacques was still tending his financial wounds from that expensive fling.

Dating a model was the lowest thing on Sabre's list. If he had a list. He did not have a list of characteristics that made up the perfect woman for him.

And yet, as he slid his hand into Cady's grasp and gave it a reassuring squeeze across the stick shift, he realized she would most definitely top that nonexistent list. She made him feel…not alone. Noticed. More alive, if that were possible. Sure, he lived for the moment and went on daring adventures, living life to the fullest. But something was missing.

Or had been missing.

Mon Dieu, could Cady be the woman who might fill that empty place in his heart? Did he require an outside source to do that for him? No, every man or woman was the creator of their own happiness. He knew that much. But having another soul who cared about him, loved him, was important to him. No man wanted to be alone forever. Was he ready to allow someone into his life on a more permanent basis?

Anything was possible. But he couldn't show Cady the respect she deserved by keeping the date with Ashayari. Yet, refusing the date would disappoint Pierre. And one of these days—someday—he'd finally earn the respect he desired from Pierre. Get the old man to simply notice him. Maybe even pat him on the back.

Sabre may never stop striving for that goal. To think such a thing saddened him, yet he knew it was an intangible goal that would forever hang just out of his grasp.

"You get a text?" he asked to fill the silence.

"My boss. He wants me to call him. I will… soon." Tucking away her phone, she peered out the window. "I love that some of the streets have cobblestones. Paris is perfectly juxtaposed with the old and the modern. I can imagine riding in a wobbly carriage down one of these streets. Must have been a nightmare trying to hold that wobbly Jell-O fruitcake you were bringing to Mom's for Christmas dinner."

"Do you think they had Jell-O back in the time of carriages?"

"Well, it was aspic or something weird made from beef hooves."

Sabre gaped at her.

"Really. Aspic is meat Jell-O. I've browsed old recipes online. What do you think gelatin is made from?"

"Beef hooves?" he wondered in disgust.

"You got it."

"Remind me never to take an assignment that

reveals the photographic history of traditional folk recipes. Let's stick with the ham sandwiches."

He maneuvered the car into the garage beneath his building and parked. Before opening the door, he peeked in the bag to study the macaron assortment. He offered the chocolate one to Cady.

"But you like the chocolate ones the best," she protested, but weakly. "They were the only flavor you chose at the buffet."

"That you know that about me makes me happy." He held up the small cookie as if a great treasure he'd just discovered. "I want you to have this one. My greatest sacrifice for the woman I adore," he said dramatically.

With a laugh, she leaned in and took a bite from the macaron. "You're a charmer." Her smile dropped and she grabbed the door pull. "But save some for the model."

With that, she stepped outside, leaving him sitting behind the wheel with a half-eaten macaron. He sighed and tossed the macaron into the open bag on the passenger seat. "She is upset."

And usually with his past relationships, he'd feel it had come to an end when the woman showed dissatisfaction or downright anger with him. Time to part ways. Rather, he walked away no matter the woman's opinion of their relationship status.

Very well, he was a runner. A man who ran

away from women. A man who ran away from his family. A man who filled his empty heart with adventure and a wild life of abandon. Because if he ran away, then he didn't have to stand there and feel his heart break due to lacking attention, of being overlooked. Of feeling not loved as much as his brothers.

The challenges of family.

"Indeed," he muttered.

Yet, Cady was different. The emotional connection they had developed meant the world to him. It was like nothing he'd ever experienced. And even though he knew that she was a people pleaser, that she went out of her way to make others happy, he saw that she had allowed some of that control to slip away over the past week. And he wanted her to know that she could have any life she desired. She could put herself first. But he couldn't do that with her angry at him. He wanted to fight for her acceptance.

But if he had to fight for it, would it truly be genuine?

CHAPTER FIFTEEN

CADY ACTUALLY MOANED out loud as the sweet Gruyère cheese melted on her tongue. Crisp bits of baguette and ham sliced so thin she felt sure she could see through it put any previous sandwich she had eaten to shame. French cooking had won her heart. How to fill her fridge with this food upon her return to her real life?

But the real question wasn't about food at all. Or that Sabre seemed to be going out of his way to cater to her. Offering her more wine after but a few sips. Asking if the food was the right temperature. Asking her advice on what she thought about changing some of the penthouse decor.

He was placating her. And she knew it because she was a pro when it came to pleasing others. He knew she was angry with him. Not exactly angry. Just…disappointed. In herself. Because the man had every right to take out whomever he pleased. The way she'd reacted to his actions was not her usual accepting, accommodating self.

And that made her realize something. Compliant Cady had decided she'd had enough. No more pleasing others to make herself feel good. Because if this is what it felt like on the receiving end? Ugh.

But this revelation, and thus her anger, was new territory she wasn't sure how to navigate. The wisest move would be to simply hash it out, talk to him, tell him her feelings.

What *were* her feelings? Did she feel as though Sabre was her man and how dare he date another woman?

Yes. On both parts. And he'd come right out and said they were a couple with his brother as a witness. They'd enjoyed a week getting to know one another, growing closer, having great sex. But a week did not make for a real relationship. Did it?

It could, she thought, as she pushed her plate away and lifted the wine goblet. It really could. Sabre was the only man who had ever made her care, made her step beyond her compliance and think in new terms. In ways of what *she* wanted, what was best for her, what would make her happy as opposed to always trying to please others.

And that was something her mother could never claim to grasp.

But on the other hand, she had to admit that part of her must like the fact that he had so much money. Seriously. Who would not? He could show her the world. Make her life so wondrous.

Was she jealous of his billions? Of course!

And yet, he gave so much of it away. And to great causes. And that made her embarrassed by her jealousy. And it wasn't as though she would ever ask him for any of it, expect him to give her money. As her mom expected from her suitors. Cady couldn't even imagine what she would do had she the billions he had.

Travel, for sure. Eat all the food. Try all the clothes. Get herself the biggest, deepest tub she could fit in her tiny house…

Argh! This *thing* between them had become complicated.

Sabre silently got up and cleared the dishes from the table, taking his time rinsing them in the sink while she moved to the sofa to gaze at the Eiffel Tower alive with lights. Yet, she wondered how long it would take before a person, who lived in this penthouse, to tire of the nightly light show and just want to pull the blankets over her head and get some sleep.

Already moved yourself into his penthouse, eh?

No. And really, this place did not feel like a home. And Sabre knew that as well. But he couldn't admit it to himself. Cady had seen him come alive while showing her through his grandfather's mansion. That was his real home. Or, at least, it could be the perfect landing pad for when his job allowed him to return to Paris now and then.

"How many days out of the year do you travel?" she asked, still gazing at the Iron Lady, the wine goblet empty and wobbling between her fingers.

He walked up to her and offered his hand, which she took. In her slightly softened-by-alcohol state, she would never refuse a handsome Frenchman's hand. But that didn't mean she was going to stuff her anger under the table regarding his upcoming date and give him a free pass.

They sat on the sofa angled toward the window and he turned his body to face hers. "I've never kept track of my travel days," he said, "but I would guess eighty percent of the year."

"That is a lot of travel."

He shrugged. "It is my life."

"So is the other twenty percent spent here in Paris?"

"Yes. Though I own a palazzo in Venice. And there is my apartment in Taiwan. I do like to take a vacation, if you will. Just relax and read for days sometimes."

"Really?" Reading? Now this was a new side to the man. Which only proved that she didn't know him at all. And, oh, how she wanted to discover everything she could about him. "What do you like to read?"

"Everything. Natural history. Travel journals. Mysteries. And I shouldn't admit this, but I do love it when a story has a good romance in it."

"Admit it," she challenged. "A woman likes when a man shows his vulnerabilities."

He bowed his head. "So you liked to see me in my *grand-père*'s home today? At my most vulnerable?"

"I didn't mean it that way. But, yes, it was good to see what sets your soul on fire. All the cameras, the trinkets you picked up for your grandfather on your travels and the memories you shared with me? That was you opening your heart to me. Made me feel like you trust me."

"I do trust you." He trailed a finger down her hair and tucked it behind her ear. He smelled so delicious. His body heat lured her closer. Could she couch her anger for just a few kisses? "Like I've never trusted a woman before. Cady, you must know that you are special to me."

His words sounded good. In theory. But were they simply sweet nothings?

He bent to try to catch her gaze, but she was finding it difficult to meet his eyes. Too heart-wrenching, knowing this thing they had could only go in one direction. And that meant her, on a plane, flying west to Vegas.

All of a sudden, her phone rang. She checked the screen, not intending to answer. But… "My boss."

"You should take it, *oui*?"

Yes, she should. But they were having a conversation. A serious one that could mean so much if they finally talked things out.

"Take it," he insisted. "With the time difference, you must take the opportunity now before it gets late."

True. Walking to the window to look at the Eiffel Tower, Cady answered the call. Her boss apologized for bothering her on vacation, but said it was important to let her know that Lisa had given her notice and that Victory would be looking for another client liaison to replace her. He felt Cady would fit the position. Could she think about it and give him an answer when she returned to Las Vegas?

Overwhelmed with a gush of happiness, she turned to face Sabre, but he'd wandered in the kitchen, his back to her. No way to share the momentous moment with a silent smile and perhaps a wink from him.

"Uh," she suddenly remembered to speak, "yes, I appreciate you telling me that. I… That sounds great. I will give it some thought. I should be back in a few days. Thank you."

She clicked off and clutched the phone to her

chest. It was happening! She had just been offered the promotion she desired. A raise and a chance to travel the world. Whoo-hoo!

And yet, when Sabre finally did turn to face her, she met his gaze across the room. And her smile dropped. As did her heart. Another swear word sounded in her brain. A really bad one. Here she stood. A man she'd consider giving up everything for on one side. And across the ocean, a dream job awaited.

"Cady?" he prompted. "Are you okay? Is it your mother?"

She shook her head. "It was my boss. He…" Softly, she said, "I have to fly home tomorrow, Sabre. So I can be back to work on Monday. My boss just offered me a position as a client liaison."

"That's wonderful, Cady." He crossed the room and touched her lips, and when she thought he would kiss her, he didn't. Instead, he looked lost in his thoughts. Drowning in some inner argument. To ask her to stay or simply allow her to leave? She wasn't even sure herself, how she'd want him to answer that one.

"I don't want you to go, Cady. I need you. I will do whatever I can to make you stay."

The word *need* scared her. Especially coming from a man who, on the surface, exuded confidence.

"Sabre, I don't want you to need me."

Because all her life she had catered to other's needs. Pleasing those who needed.

What do you need? I can make it happen. Go ask Cady for whatever you need.

Need, need, need!

"If you do not want me to need you," he began, "then what is it you want from me? And please tell me you want something from me. Anything."

"Sabre, I..." Dare she? It would be like diving into the depths. And no light at the surface to ensure she made it safely to the surface. It would require she rip open her heart and show him her own needs.

"Cady?"

"I want you to love me," she blurted, much against the part of her that desired to cling to the shore. But she had made the dive. He had taught her to do that.

"I do love you," he said.

"You do?"

Maybe she could make it to the surface? But. No. She must be very clear with him. Because for once in her life, she understood what would make her happy.

"Sabre, when you say you need me, and that means you love me, that's...well, that's wrong. Needing me is not loving me. You're telling the queen of fulfilling other's needs you need me? Ugh."

"I understand. I don't want it to mean that to you."

She sighed. "Do you know what I want from you?"

"Tell me."

She touched his mouth. His moustache tickled her skin. He was perfection. In ways beyond the exterior. The man truly did fit into her soul in ways she could not begin to comprehend. "Sabre, I want you to love me wildly and without promises."

"How do you know my love is not that exactly?"

"Well..."

"Cady, you want the wild love from me? I have shown you nothing but freedom and daring." He bracketed her face with his hands. Those pale brown eyes were so true. "The question is, do *you* love me?"

"Well, I—"

He held up a finger to pause her confession. "Arcadia Burton, I think you love the wildness I am. The wildness I can give you. A wildness you will never dare grasp. Not completely."

His words struck her in the heart. True words. Sabre had a life that she craved. A wild and free life. Follow him across the world on his travels? Yes, please.

But, no. How could she possibly allow herself that freedom? She had a job back home. A new and better-paying job. And a mother who needed her. And did she actually believe she belonged in Sabre's world of adventure, billions and fast cars?

"I think..." she started, not really thinking through what she would say, but it was too hard to not speak, otherwise she'd cry. "...we've been using one another for selfish reasons."

He opened his mouth to reply but she touched his lips again, quieting him.

"You got something from me that has been missing from your life. Yes?"

He closed his eyes and nodded. "*Oui.* You restored in me a confidence I had surely thought lost."

"And I'm doing the same. Taking advantage of the freedom you can offer me. But it's just a fantasy, Sabre. It can never be real."

"I...don't know what to say to that." He glanced out the window. The Eiffel Tower twinkled.

She had spoken the truth. *Her* truth. And it hurt to put it out there. But it shouldn't hurt. Why did the truth have to hurt?

"I have fallen in love with you," Cady said softly. "But you know I don't belong in your world. I can't compete with a model. Even if she is, as you say, just a favor to your father. Nor would I want to follow you from country to country like a pack dog expected to take notes and bring you your snacks on cue." A cruel mistruth, but she needed some segue to allow her to step away.

To sever ties.

"Cady, I—" He hooked his elbow on the back of the sofa and leaned in. "The job offer is incredible. I should not dare to insist you refuse it. But...what if I asked you to stay with me? I think your fear is of taking a big leap. Well, I want you to leap even higher. Move in with me."

That was a surprise, and while it made her heart flutter with hope, it also snapped a finger at that red flag.

"Sabre, what we have is amazing right now. But refusing the job offer and moving in with you? It feels like a desperate plea from an uncertain man. And even if I did move in with you? What if one month, or even a year down the road, we break up? I'd be left stranded in a foreign country with nothing. I can't do that. I won't sacrifice my—"

"Yes, your security. Your careful world." He rubbed a hand over his head and stood, gesturing outward as he said, "I don't want to have to fight for your attention, Cady. It feels too familiar. And that feeling hurts. So..." Now he gestured to the door. "If you do not have trust in me, then you must leave."

That was abrupt. But Cady couldn't see a means to stay. They'd both put out their feelings for one another. They loved one another. And yet, the distance between them was impossible.

For her, at least.

She nodded and stood, collecting her jacket. Cady walked out of the room, heading for the guest room to collect her things. She'd spend the night at a hotel and book a flight to fly out tomorrow. He was offering her an easy out.

He's offering you freedom if you stay.

How cruel that she did not dare claim that freedom.

When the front door shut, Sabre closed his eyes. Had he just allowed Cady to walk out of his life? For good? What a fool was he?

She was right. About all of it.

Well, no. He did not like that she'd called herself a pack dog. Is that how she had felt following him on assignment in Finland? He must correct her thinking on that. And hell, a promotion at work? He should not have suggested she consider refusing. It was something she desired. And Cady must have whatever she desired. But she simply could not see beyond her self-imposed walls. Walls built to protect her heart. Walls he had thought he'd broken down.

But in truth, they had been using one another to fill holes in their lives. And while Sabre couldn't quite figure why that should be so wrong, he felt a hurt rise from his gut. A familiar hurt.

Cady had walked away from him. And he was terribly accustomed to that feeling of abandonment.

He picked up his phone and tapped the message app. There were no texts from Grand-père. Sabre's heart dropped. Never had he needed the old man more than right now.

CHAPTER SIXTEEN

AN HOUR LATER, Sabre opened the door in hopes of finding Cady standing there with her big smile and hopeful shoulders. Instead, there stood Pierre d'Aramitz. The man offered a shrug and held a brown envelope before him.

"Pierre?" Sabre felt sure he'd never once been in this penthouse in the three years he'd owned it.

Had he been thinking how much he'd needed his *grand-père*? And now, here was someone so opposite the kind and guiding force who had molded his life and made him the man he had become today.

"Might I come in? I…er…found this in the few things that Jacques and I had rescued from Gaston's home and forgot to give it to you when you were over the other day."

Thinking to simply take the envelope and then usher him away, Sabre's shoulders dropped. Yet, his heart leaped forward. Something very Cady-like bloomed in him. Here was a moment alone with Pierre. And as he'd learned from the last few days spent with Cady, he must take any of these moments that he could. Enjoy them. He'd figure it all out later.

"Come in, then. Whiskey?"

"Uh, no. I'm attending a function tonight with a friend. Want to be in top form."

"A function?" Sabre paused before the sofa and gestured Pierre seat himself.

Pierre took a moment to look around, taking in the room and the view of the Eiffel Tower.

"Yes, a small affair with Melanie's family. I'm seeing someone, you know?"

"I didn't know that. Serious?" Sabre sat. It felt strange to get some personal information from Pierre. But not unwelcome.

"Oh, I don't think I'll ever remarry." Pierre gestured over his shoulder as he turned to sit on the chair opposite the sofa. "Nice view. I never tire of that monstrosity."

"I am home so rarely," Sabre said, "that I never tire of it, either. So, Melanie?"

"She is lovely. A former actress. She did a film directed by Luc Besson. Don't worry, she won't replace your mother."

Sabre's mouth compressed as he bowed his head. He and Pierre had never discussed his mother. Why, even between his siblings it had merely been a few random moments of wonder over her.

Do you remember her? Was she nice?

"I don't even remember her," he said calmly. "I was so young."

Pierre bowed his head. "Pauline was my world."

Something loosened in Sabre's stiff posture. Never had he heard such emotion in Pierre's voice. Nor had he been told anything about Pierre and Pauline's life together. "Tell me?"

"I wish that you could have known her well," Pierre offered. "She loved you. All her boys. Well, Blaise was just six months old when she died. Her death was…difficult for me. I—" Pierre sighed heavily "—apologize for the way things went after. You slipped away from me. And I allowed it. I should have tried harder to be a father to you."

Sabre didn't know what to say. An apology after decades of ignoring him? Certainly, he had never thought in terms of how difficult it must have been for Pierre after Pauline's death. Because he'd been five at the time. All he'd known was that suddenly the soft, loving woman who had cared for him was gone. And his world then revolved around maids and nannies. And eventually his *grand-père*.

"When Gaston saw how I was handling things—which was not so well—he started to come over. I had my hands full with Blaise, and Jacques was old enough that he spent most of his time with his friends. So Gaston focused on you," Pierre said.

"He took me for walks in the park." Sabre smiled to recall chasing ducks and eating gelatos. "It was a good time."

"You two bonded in ways that made me jealous."

Saber lifted his head.

Pierre offered a shrug. "It is true, much as it is terrible to admit. And at the time, I thought to myself, well, one of my sons is getting the attention he requires. So I was thankful for Gaston spending time with you. Only when you began to resent me did I regret it."

"I've never resented you, Pierre."

Pierre sighed. "I should have never accepted you calling me by name."

"It is who you are."

"True. But please know that I have always loved you, Sabre. And always will. I just thought it necessary to say it to you. With the passing of my father, I've been looking at life differently. What is important to me? I've always thought it was family, but we all know it has been my work. I want to change that. I will try."

"Family is important," Sabre said. "But what is more important is surrounding yourself with people you love. And if you cannot be surrounded, then having one important person to notice you can change your world."

Instantly, the image of Cady came to mind. He loved her. Where was she right now? He must get her back in his life. And no missing text from Gaston would make it any easier. This was something he had to do on his own.

"I hope you will allow me to stumble my way back into your life," Pierre said. "In some form or other."

Would he allow such a thing? It would certainly feel awkward to have Pierre closer and—might he ever call him Dad? Perhaps take him on one of his photography excursions? The thought put a smile on Sabre's face.

"I would like that," he said. "We can stumble around one another."

"*Bien*. So I wanted you to have this." He handed Sabre the envelope. "That was stuffed in an album in the attic. My father had saved all our wedding photos. Pauline was never one to hang photos in the house. But I think you'll like to have that one."

Sabre pulled out from the envelope a large color photo. It featured a woman with long dark hair holding a newborn baby up by her face. She gazed into the baby's alert eyes. A strand of her hair fell across the baby's white blanket.

"This is me and… Mom?"

"Just hours after you were born. Wasn't she lovely?"

He traced a finger over the photo. So young, and beautiful. And the look on her face was so joyous. He nodded, finding he had to swallow to keep back a swell of emotion.

Pierre stood and wandered to the window, his back to Sabre. "She called you her wild one. It was because of your hair."

He did have an awful lot of black hair that stuck up as if a windstorm had swept him from below.

"She perhaps had precognition of what you would become," Pierre said over his shoulder. "Wildly adventuring across the world. Not to be tamed. Always seeking wonder. I'm proud of you, Sabre."

"You…you are?" A tug inside his chest broached his careful monitoring and a teardrop dropped onto his cheek. He quickly swiped it away.

"I am. And I know whatever your future brings will be because it is what you have created and brought to yourself. Who knows? You and Ashayari may hit it off."

"We won't." Sabre set the photo on the coffee table and stood. He stepped up to the window beside Pierre. "I'm going to ask Blaise if he will escort Ashayari to the party. I did tell you I've a woman in my life."

Pierre studied him. "Serious?"

"I want it to be."

Pierre nodded, taking that in. "Does she make you happy?"

"Every moment I am with her. I don't want her to leave Paris, but she may be on her way back to the States as we speak."

"Then why are you standing here talking to me?" Pierre's smile grew.

"Exactly. Thank you, Pierre, for the photo. And…for telling me those things. It changes a lot. Or it will. I think it's time we started acting like a father and son, *oui*?"

"*Oui*."

When Pierre held out his hand, as if to shake, the old man looked at the movement, glanced up to Sabre, then held out his arms. Taking him into a hug, slapping him across the shoulders, the twosome embraced, for the first time in a long time. It was brief, a little awkward. But it meant something to Sabre.

A new beginning.

"I'm off to get ready for the party," Pierre said as he started for the door. "Have you decided what to do with the mansion? If you sell it, let me know. I may have the bronze statues taken out and put up for auction."

"You can do that no matter what I decide. But

I will let you know." Sabre opened the door for Pierre. As he left, he called after him, "I love you!

Pierre paused, turned around and nodded. "I love you too, *mon fils*."

Stepping back inside and closing the door, Sabre leaned against the door. That had been odd, unexpected and… "Great."

Cady stood behind a line of tourists checking in at a hotel on the Rue de Rivoli. A glance out the front doors spied the neon-lit Ferris wheel across the street in the Tuileries Garden. The City of Lights thrived all around her. Unaware how tattered her heart felt. That every step she took felt so unstable she might topple as if her cross-country skis had hit an ice patch.

She was headed back to Las Vegas. To accept a new position that would allow her to meet new people and occasionally travel to foreign countries. It was a dream come to life. And yet, her heart didn't beat with a giddy pace as she thought it should for such a thrilling life change.

She had experienced the kind of happiness that made her heart dance. With Sabre. When she'd not thought about trying to please him, but rather had existed in the moment. He'd done that for her. Had shown her what life could offer.

And she'd walked away from it.

Well. It wasn't as though he'd given her a solid

offer to stay with him. A guarantee that a year down the road they'd still be together and life would be fabulous. There had been no guarantees.

Sabre wasn't that kind of man. He lived in the moment.

Cady lived to please others. And once at home, her mom would toss out complaints about how Cady had thrown away a good thing. A billionaire! She could have had it all. And taken her mother along for the ride.

She wasn't sure how long she could last with her mother as a roommate. Now she understood why she had survived as a child. Because her mother hadn't always been there. They worked best when they were together but not. Family, yet distant enough to not get on one another's nerves.

Cady had never felt comfortable spending a lot of time around any specific person. Until Sabre.

She already missed that sexy French voice whispering to her as he nuzzled into her hair and slid his naked body alongside hers. They had only made love that one night. And morning. She'd never stop yearning for his body. Never.

"What have I done?" she declared to no one but herself.

Had she actually walked out of Sabre's life? Never to see him again? What had become of Careful Cady? Walking away from an unresolved fight didn't sit right with her. They'd ended things on what should have been a high note. Both of them had confessed their love for one another.

He'd said he *needed* her.

She had always equated need with love. All her life she'd substituted the word *love* for *need.* Made life easier to navigate and survive. But now she knew there was more. Beyond need.

There was real love. And even though he'd used the word *need*, Cady knew that Sabre loved her. For real.

And she loved him.

Sure, they had only known one another a short time, but time didn't matter when her heart knew. Sabre had changed her life.

So why wasn't she willing to embrace that change? To take what she desired?

I don't want to have to fight for your attention.

Those words he'd said had grown into an earworm in her brain. She could not stop hearing them. Sabre's voice had ached. And now she realized what it had meant. He'd fought for attention all his life. From his father. His family. The only one who had ever made him feel loved was now dead. And then she had entered his life and, yes, he'd said something about feeling seen by her. That he loved her.

She loved him.

"Cady, what are you doing? Don't hurt him like that."

"Madame?" The woman behind the reception desk prompted Cady.

Cady took a step toward the desk. Then stopped. This was not her. She did not hurt people. She was the one who made sure others were happy.

She again glanced at the front doors.

The couple behind her slipped around her, taking her place in line at the desk.

What waited for her back in Las Vegas? A new job that would pay the bills and allow her a little extra. Travel, but not with anyone she knew or cared about. A mother who would never change her careless ways. One step up from her simple life. A life that worked for her. But it didn't fill her heart with wonder or make her sigh in fascination.

Sabre wanted to give her that.

And what if they did give it a try, decided to do the couple thing, and then broke up a month down the road? A year? She truly would be left with nothing, because in order to stay with Sabre she'd have to quit her job, sell her house…

Her mom *was* staying there now.

"It could work," she murmured.

Was she prepared to sacrifice this new opportunity to become a client liaison for the unknown?

A smile made its way onto Cady's face. And this time when prompted to step to the reception desk, she shook her head. And headed toward the doors.

CHAPTER SEVENTEEN

SABRE PACED THE PENTHOUSE. Where in Paris might Cady have gone? He had texted her, but received no reply. Might she already be in the air, on her way back to the States?

Why had he let her walk away from him? Was he mad?

The one good thing that had entered his life was now gone.

He'd meant it when he'd offered to let her move in with him. He wanted Cady in his life. If that was for the rest of his life, then great! If they only lasted a month or a year, as she'd suggested, then he would be happy for the time they were given. They could never know the future.

Should he have proposed to her? Made it more permanent?

Sabre shook his head. It felt too fast. But keeping Cady in his life did not feel fast. It felt like the only way he could continue to breathe.

"I have to find her."

Grabbing a jacket, he rushed to the door. He'd

call her again in the car. Opening the door, he walked right into Cady. He caught her in his embrace. Their bodies fitted together.

Made for one another.

He cupped her head and kissed her. Long. Deeply. He wanted to say sorry, and I love you, and let's talk all at once. But mostly he wanted to say we are right for one another.

When he broke the kiss and led her across the threshold, he asked, "You came back?"

"You were just leaving?" she countered.

"To find you. I was wrong, Cady. Whatever I said, I'm sorry."

"Please don't apologize for speaking your truth. We were both truthful. And I wasn't able to listen beyond my self-imposed boundaries. I'm the one who is sorry. I shouldn't have walked out on you like I did. I don't want you to fight for my attention. You have it whenever you want it, Sabre. And… I see you."

He bowed his head to hers and kissed her nose. Those words were like balm to the ache he'd felt for years. And he believed them. Because he had been witness to her seeing him. To learning him. To knowing him. She cared about Sabre d'Aramitz.

"I know you do," he said softly.

"And I'm not my mom," she said. "I don't want you for your money."

"I know that."

"It's just, this is a big step for me. And you scared me when you said I could stay with you. It felt... desperate."

"I didn't mean it to come out that way, but I realize now that it did. And I also realize that asking you to say no to that job offer is very selfish on my part. But the invitation stands. I want you to move in with me, Cady. You are my woman. I know my *grand-père* would have loved you. And if you do choose to stay with me, just know that I plan to move to the mansion. This penthouse is not my home."

"I know that as well. Although the bathtub..."

"We can have it moved to the mansion."

"Really? We?" She bounced a little. "So, it's as easy as that?"

"It can be." He kissed her again. Hers was a mouth he would never tire of kissing. A body that would always lure him deeper into bliss. "You know I am not a man who thinks on things too much. I leap. Can you make a leap into my life?" Studying her green eyes, her entire face brightened, growing as luminous as his heart felt. "I love you, Cady."

"I love you, too." And with a deciding tilt of her head, she said, "I want to do this. In fact..." She walked into the living area and turned to him. "I did a thing."

He eyed her curiously. "A thing?"

Teasing a fingertip against her teeth, she shrugged. "I quit my job. Said no to the new job as well."

Yes! She was committing to this stay with him.

"And… I called my mom and told her I was going to stay in Paris for a while and that she could have my house. That is, she'll have to pay the mortgage. Which I know she can't do for too long. I'll have to find a job to pay the mortgage while I'm here. Because you never know what might happen between us."

"Let me buy the house for you and your mother," Sabre said. "Please?"

"I couldn't."

"But you can. You just have to say *oui*."

She smiled and shook her head. "I understand that it is something which would make you happy to do for me."

"It would. And—"

She pressed a finger to his mouth. "And, yes, I know you can afford it. Let's take this one step at a time, shall we? Mom will be okay for a few months."

"I see. You need a safety net in case you think I will toss you out?"

"Maybe? We can't know what the future will bring."

"We can't. But I will try my hardest to ensure you wish to remain with me and not regret turning down that job."

"That job did include travel."

"Loving me includes travel."

"Oh, yeah?" She teased the tip of her tongue

along her lower lip. "But I don't want to get in your way if you're working."

"You'll know when I must focus and when you can accompany me. This will work, Cady." He took her hands and danced her to the window overlooking the Eiffel Tower. "And when I am not working, we will perfect our tango, yes?"

"I'm game. But what about a job for me? I get that you're offering to let me stay here on your dollar, but I like to work. To feel needed."

"You'll figure something out. An online job should be doable. There's always the other option. You can be my assistant."

"I enjoyed that."

"And I would not order you around like a pack dog."

"I shouldn't have put it that way. I was angry when I said that. I loved assisting you, Sabre. You're right. I'll figure something out."

"I'm very impressed, Cady. You've just embraced a big change."

"I have. But when I was standing in the hotel, waiting to reserve a room, my heart wouldn't allow me to do so. It told me I was in the wrong place." She kissed him. "Anywhere you are feels like the right place. Like a touchstone."

"You make me very happy, Cady."

"And you make me want to say yes to everything."

EPILOGUE

Six months later...

CADY BURTON HAD said yes to the billionaire Sabre d'Aramitz.

She had followed him to Morocco to photograph a waterfall framed by lush forest, to Berlin to witness a youth gang determined to clean up the remaining Berlin Wall of graffiti. Greenland had been a kick. Blue icebergs! And who knew she'd be so daring as to scuba dive on the Great Barrier Reef. They'd returned to Paris for a weekend during which she'd helped him to move some of his things from the penthouse into the mansion. As well, she'd had her clothing shipped from Vegas to the mansion. And she'd moved the photograph of the monkey to the wall in the bathroom.

She had moved in with Sabre! And she didn't regret a moment of it.

The life she'd left behind in Las Vegas was

an old chapter. Her mother had gratefully taken Cady's house off her hands and recently mentioned her date with a man she'd met at a poker table. Cady expected marriage number five within the year. It was her mother's way. Might she let the house go up for sale? The thought to keep it as a safety backup was no longer so important.

On to her new chapter. One that involved a man who adored her. And saying yes to adventure. She'd already experienced so many new places!

Dubai had been an amazing adventure. The heather fields of Scotland had made her long for an ancient castle set at the top of a craggy hill. Sabre had offered to buy her one. She...was seriously considering that offer. And remaining on board the boat while Sabre had dived to photograph stingrays off the coast of Australia had made her top-ten list. A list that would continue to be sorted, switched out and possibly grow to a top one hundred.

Who knew what the future would bring?

Lots of travel, for sure. She was up for that. Learning a new language, of course. No way could she live in Paris and not learn French. Accepting that all her wants would be catered to at Sabre's whim was the hard part. Allowing herself to be pampered, pleasured and treated as if she deserved it all.

But she was willing to take that journey because, somehow, she knew Sabre would not overdo it by showering her with ridiculous things like furs and other useless material items. He was a man who showed his love through action.

And right now, the gesture he made with a crook of his finger and a wink made her heart so full she beamed at him. Cady walked across the field of black volcanic rock toward him. It was midnight in Mauna Kea, Hawaii, and they'd driven up to the highest peak to view the spectacular night sky. Above Cady's head, the entire galaxy burst in stars. They twinkled in all colors against the velvet azure night.

Sabre kissed her on the forehead. "You enjoying yourself, my beautiful wonder?"

"Absolutely! I've never seen so many stars. There must be bajillions of them."

"Which one do you want?" He studied the sky for a moment, then said, "If you could have any star in the sky, tell me which one you'd choose."

"Hmm…"

He was always asking her stuff like that. Generally, it followed with him buying her a pretty dress or donating to a local turtle shelter so the one she had fallen in love with could live another one or two hundred years. Or even collecting sales pamphlets for Scottish castles.

Perusing the sky for a moment, she then pointed.

"That one there, just to the right of that really bright one."

He pointed. "That one?"

"A bit to the right. It's got a sort of purple tinge to it."

"This one." His fingertip landed right over the star she wanted. "Got it!" He clasped his fingers into a fist, then brought it down between the two of them and held it before her as if a child hiding something. "Do you want to take a look?"

Wiggling her shoulders, she leaned in and touched his fingers. She loved his hands. They knew how to make her cry out in ecstasy or when to stroke her hair gently as she fell asleep after a long day. Peeling back one of his fingers she prepared herself to marvel over the invisible star when—

Cady let out a surprised chirp. She looked up at her lover. Then back at the diamond ring laying on his palm. "Sabre?"

He went down on one knee before her under the midnight sky sparkling with bajillions of stars and held up the ring. "Arcadia Burton, will you marry me?"

Tears rolling down her eyes, she could only nod. And then her voice found its way out, "Yes! I love you! Yes!"

He rose and fitted the ring onto her finger, then pulled her into a kiss that bowed her gently backward. Cady's foot left the ground. Her heart raced with joy. And above them, the sky winked in approval.

She had said yes, not only to the billionaire but to a wondrous life filled with adventure, joy and love.

* * * * *

If you enjoyed this story, check out these other great reads from Michele Renae

The CEO and the Single Dad Cinderella's Second Chance in Paris

Available now!